"Well, now, I'm normally not one to interfere in other people's business...but it appears to me the woman doesn't want to get into your car, and here in Texas, we don't force women against their will."

The big bruiser glared at Mac. "This is none of your concern. I suggest you get back in your truck and leave unless you want to deal with me."

Mac risked a glance at the woman and his heart skipped a solid beat. Maybe two. It was the fierce expression in her eyes that snagged his attention.

She was afraid, but she was also full of determination.

Mac hoisted the rifle higher. "It seems to me we have a problem, 'cause I can't just let you take off with the lady if she doesn't want to go."

The woman struggled and the big guy tightened his hold on her arm. He lifted his pistol and pointed it straight at Mac. The woman closed her eyes and her lips started moving.

"I'd rather not leave a dead body on the side of the road, but it's your choice," the pistol holder said, his finger on the trigger.

Liz Shoaf resides in North Carolina on a beautiful fifty-acre farm. She loves writing and adores dog training, and her husband is very tolerant of the amount of time she invests in both her avid interests. Liz also enjoys spending time with family, jogging and singing in the choir at church whenever possible. To find out more about Liz, you can visit and contact her through her website, www.lizshoaf.com, or email her at phelpsliz1@gmail.com.

Books by Liz Shoaf

Love Inspired Suspense

Betrayed Birthright
Identity: Classified
Holiday Mountain Conspiracy
Texas Ranch Sabotage
Texas Ranch Refuge

Visit the Author Profile page at LoveInspired.com.

TEXAS RANCH REFUGE

LIZ SHOAF

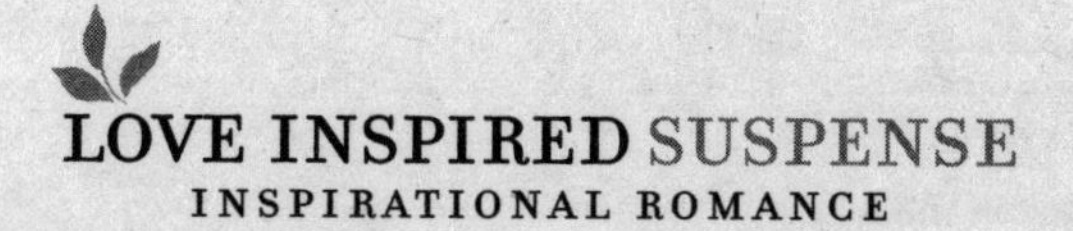

LOVE INSPIRED® SUSPENSE
INSPIRATIONAL ROMANCE

Recycling programs for this product may not exist in your area.

ISBN-13: 978-1-335-55476-5

Texas Ranch Refuge

This edition published by arrangement with Harlequin Books S.A.

For questions and comments about the quality of this book, please contact us at CustomerService@Harlequin.com.

Love Inspired
22 Adelaide St. West, 40th Floor
Toronto, Ontario M5H 4E3, Canada
www.LoveInspired.com

Printed in U.S.A.

Have not I commanded thee? Be strong and of a good courage; be not afraid, neither be thou dismayed: for the Lord thy God is with thee whithersoever thou goest.

—*Joshua* 1:9

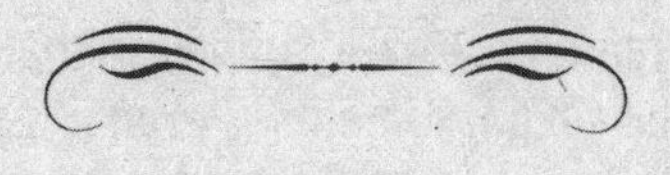

I simply have to dedicate this book to several of the best trainers I know: Dudley, Erin, Julie and Lynne. You have limitless patience with both the humans and the dogs and I appreciate you all more than you know.

And to all the trainers out there who spend their lives training search-and-rescue canines so that countless lives may be saved, sometimes even in dangerous situations. Bravo! To both the trainers and those very special and unique animals.

ONE

Slumped in her chair, surrounded by her small cubicle in an empty office at the prestigious Kale, Kale & Johnston law firm, Liv Calloway glanced at the secondhand Rolex she'd gifted herself for her twenty-seventh birthday. It was almost 7:00 p.m., and the place had a skeletal feel. She found it a tad unnerving, just as she did every time she worked late, which was a lot. She welcomed the voices floating into the large room from the corridor. As they neared the door to her office, she recognized Mr. Kale's voice.

"You're sure you covered all your tracks?" Mr. Kale asked.

Liv wondered briefly if she should let her boss know she was sitting within hearing distance, but surely, even though the building was presumed empty, he wouldn't be having a private conversation in the corridor.

"Yes, sir!" a deep voice Liv recognized answered. A voice that made chills race up her spine. It was one of two men privately employed by Mr. Kale, not a member of the firm. She'd seen them around the office but generally steered clear of the two tough-looking men.

"Good. Now that we've removed Burton from the equation, Mr. Stevenson will be free and clear."

Every bone in Liv's body stiffened, and she forgot to breathe. She'd been honored when she was chosen to assist in their client Mr. Stevenson's defense. But after the only witness, Mr. Burton, had been killed in a hit-and-run just the day before, she knew it would be dismissed. And based on her boss's words, it hadn't been an accident.

Her granddaddy always said nothing good ever came from eavesdropping, she thought semihysterically, and he was right. Her mind raced. If her boss and his two henchmen found her here, they might assume she had overheard their conversation, and she'd be as dead as Mr. Burton. The lights were burning brightly in the cavernous room packed with cubicles, but that wasn't unusual, as workers were always forgetting to turn them off.

Liv jerked her body down as low as she could when she heard Mr. Kale say, "Turn off those lights." They'd drawn even with her door. Her heart racing so fast she could feel her pulse thrumming in her neck, she released a slow breath when the overhead lights flickered off and the men moved on, their murmuring voices drifting away. Away from her, she thought as relief hit her in a wave so hard it almost made her dizzy.

The urge to flee overcame her, and with trembling hands, she opened her top drawer and felt around for the tiny flashlight she kept there for emergencies. Locating the object by feel, she wrapped her fingers around the cool, rounded handle and slowly, so as not to make any noise, pulled it from the drawer. Pausing, she raised herself up and peered over the top of her cubicle.

The only things lit were the emergency exit lights, so she hit the button, turning on the flashlight. She cringed when she dropped a tube of lipstick as she quickly stuffed personal items strewn across her desk into her purse. Thankfully, the carpet stifled the noise.

Her mind was racing as she slid the strap of her gently used Da Milano purse over her head and across her chest. She'd head home to Texas and call the police as soon as she left New York, giving herself a safe distance from any sort of retaliation until this was sorted out.

Creeping down the center aisle, guided by a thin beam of light, Liv stopped cold when she heard a soft rustling noise. She could see the door to the large room standing wide-open, backlit by the emergency exit light. A large shadow moved through the doorway a second before the overhead lights momentarily blinded her. When her vision cleared, her heart almost exploded out of her chest. One of Mr. Kale's men stood there with a gun in his hand and a smirk on his face.

"I thought I sensed a presence when I doused the lights. I'd advise you to come with me peacefully. Mr. Kale will want to talk to you."

Mr. Kale would likely have her "removed" just like Mr. Burton if she went with this man. She was a witness. Like prey being hunted, her instincts kicked in and she turned and fled to the other end of the room where a door led to the stairs, but the large man knocked her to the floor before she had a chance to escape, almost dislocating her shoulder when he pulled her back to her feet.

She forced herself to calm down while facing a man three times larger than her petite frame. Her skill with words was what made her a good attorney, making it one of two weapons she had at her disposal.

"I'll be glad to speak with Mr. Kale. There's no need to manhandle me," she said, tugging her arm away from his. Distracted by her calmness, he released her. Reaching into her purse, she smiled at him. "Just let me run a brush through my hair before the meeting. I must look a mess."

His expression said he didn't quite know what to think about her, so Liv reached into her purse, fingered the small can of hair spray until she had it in the correct position, lifted it out of her purse in one smooth motion and sprayed him right between the eyes.

He screamed and started clawing at his face, and she took off through the emergency exit door, down the stairs and into the street. She frantically hailed a taxi and gave the driver her address, hoping she had time to get home, pack a bag and get her dog. She'd send up a prayer, but after the death of her parents when she was a tender teenager, she'd given up on the Almighty a long time ago.

It took a bit of time to get home, but she exited the taxi in a flash and took the elevator to her apartment. Once inside, she leaned against the closed door and took deep breaths, trying to calm herself. Toenails clattered on the hardwood floor, and she forced a big smile before picking up Misty, her sweet, precious papillon dog, decked out in a cute doggie outfit.

"There's my sweet pumpkin. Did you have a good day? Did Mrs. Perkins let you out at lunch?" Misty gifted her with multiple kisses on the chin. Liv lifted her in the air. "Would you like to take a trip? You remember Kylo, don't you? At the ranch?"

Misty snorted. Her sister's dog and Misty were as different as night and day, but they'd have to get along for a little while, anyway. Liv placed her on the floor and went straight to her bedroom. There was a lot to do if she was going to be away for any length of time, including letting Mrs. Perkins know she wouldn't be home so the older lady wouldn't worry.

After stuffing her suitcase, she went online and booked a flight to Texas. The last-minute airfare cost a fortune, but she wanted out of New York as soon as possible. She quickly filled a second suitcase with everything Misty would need. On their way out the door, she decided she'd call Babette, her best friend—her only friend in New York—and let her know what was happening after she arrived in Texas.

She took a relieved breath when she procured a taxi and she and Misty were on their way to the airport.

Lifting her phone, she sought a distraction to slow her frantically beating heart. Automatically, she opened her work email to double-check that the last client email she'd sent had gone through. Her boss might be a horrible man, but she still wanted the best for her clients, especially the pro bono case she was currently working on.

Thankfully, the email had gone out before the deadline. But as she scanned the Sent box, an unfamiliar message caught her attention. Opening it, she skimmed the contents and drew a sharp breath.

It was something she hadn't sent, and it screamed

incrimination. The email showed her hiring a hit man to kill Mr. Burton. Her hands trembled when she realized Mr. Kale, or one of his associates, had set her up—probably because she was now a witness to Mr. Kale's incriminating conversation in the corridor.

She couldn't call the police now, and he knew it. It would only look as if she was fleeing the state. Leaning her head back, she closed her eyes, her only thoughts on getting to the family ranch in Texas before she ended up dead, just like poor Mr. Burton. If she wanted to live through this *and* clear her name, she'd have to find evidence proving not only her innocence, but Mr. Kale's guilt.

Mac Dolan laid a callused hand on his eight-year-old bluetick coonhound's back as he and Barnie moseyed down the two-lane highway toward Tempe Calloway's ranch. He had the driver's window down in his rusted-out ranch truck, enjoying the April temperatures that were hovering in the midseventies.

Due to his being a neighbor of the interested party, the FBI had called him to check on a small matter a couple of weeks before Easter. They'd tried to recruit him when he mustered out of the navy and he wasn't interested, but periodically, when he was bored, he'd contract out with them if they called. This case would keep him busy until his four brothers came straggling in for the holiday.

The subject of his investigation was Olivia Calloway, his former Blue Angels comrade Tempe Calloway's sister. She had been three years behind him when they were in school, and he couldn't imagine that sweet-faced kid being involved in the situation the FBI had described. Hiring a hit man to take out a witness on a case she was assisting on was a serious allegation.

The more he thought on it, maybe Olivia Calloway was up to her neck in this thing. Not that he'd ever known her that well. Back when they were young, most parents kept their kids well away from the rowdy Dolan boys.

Miss Calloway might not even be at her family ranch when he arrived. The FBI believed she was headed this way because they'd tailed her to the airport. But even if Olivia hadn't arrived yet, he'd visit with Tempe and get the lay of the land.

Barnie bayed loudly, rattling the inside of the truck, and Mac almost ran off the side of the road. When he looked ahead and saw what had caught his dog's attention, his adrenaline took a dangerous spike. He stomped on the gas for a short distance, then laid on the brake, burning rubber on the road. Grabbing a rifle mounted on the inside of the back window, he threw open the driver's door and assessed the situation at a glance, his old military training kicking in.

A petite woman dressed to the nines—or rather, who had, at some point, been dressed to the nines—was struggling against two large men trying to stuff her into the back seat of their car. Based on the condition of the wrecked car sitting on the side of the road, and the big dents on the sedan, she'd been forced off the road. On the inside, Mac was on high alert, but he casually ambled toward the two men and the woman in a nonthreatening manner.

He stared hard at the larger man, who had a bruising

grip on the woman's arm. He had big city written all over him, from his shiny dress shoes to the expensive suit he was wearing, but his crooked nose and the scar marring the right side of his not-so-handsome face told Mac he definitely wasn't an executive.

"Well, now, I'm normally not one to interfere in other people's business, but it appears to me the woman doesn't want to get into your car, and here in Texas, we don't force women against their will."

The big bruiser glared at Mac. "This is none of your concern. I suggest you get back in your truck and leave unless you want to deal with me."

The guy's words came out low and mean, and Mac released an audible sigh. He risked a glance at the woman—not caring to take his eyes off the two men but for a moment—and his heart skipped a solid beat. Maybe two. Strands of her long dirty-blond hair had escaped her ponytail, and the navy business suit she wore was sorely wrinkled. She'd also lost one shoe in the struggle, but it was the fierce expression in her eyes that snagged his attention.

She was afraid, but she was also full of determination, which would come in handy during the next few minutes. One thing he couldn't abide was a woman with no grit. She was staring at him in disbelief.

Mac moved the rifle in his hand a little higher. "Well, now, it seems to me we have a problem, 'cause I can't just let you take off with the lady if she doesn't want to go."

The woman struggled, and the big guy tightened his hold on her arm. The other guy lifted his pistol and pointed it straight at Mac. The woman closed her eyes, and her lips started moving. Mac hoped she was praying, because he was a firm believer in God.

"I'd rather not leave a dead body on the side of the road, but it's your choice," the pistol holder said, his finger on the trigger.

About that time, the worst yapping noise Mac had ever heard came from the vicinity of the woman's wrecked car. She frantically struggled against the bruiser's grip and screamed, "Misty!"

Was there another woman in the car? It would alter Mac's plans if that were the case, but his answer came when the woman's eyes filled with tears and she pleaded, "Please, if they take me, promise you'll take care of my dog."

It wouldn't come to that, but he nodded. She sniffed, then straightened her shoulders and glared at the man with a grip on her arm. "I'll go with you willingly if you let the man live. There's no need to take an innocent life."

Mac thought that was real nice of her, but not necessary. All he needed was about ten more seconds and everything would be fine. He glanced at the rear of the men's car, saw Barnie was in position and casually said, "Now, Barnie."

His dog released a baying sound loud enough to startle a grown man, and it worked. The bruiser dropped the woman's arm, the pistol holder whipped around toward the earsplitting noise and Mac flew into action.

TWO

After that horrible noise filled the air, Liv was shocked when the slow-talking cowboy moved with lightning speed. In some type of martial arts move, his entire body flew into the air, his booted foot knocking the gun out of the pistol holder's hand. The large man tried to punch the cowboy, but he whipped around and hit Liv's abductor in the nose with his fist. The large man's head jerked backward, and he stumbled, slumping against the car.

Before she could blink, she was gently shoved out of the way and the cowboy rammed the heel of his hand upward on the nose of the man who'd assuredly left bruises on her arm. It all happened so fast, it took a few seconds for Liv to realize she was free. Her first instinct was to run to her car, lock the doors and have a mini nervous breakdown, but she couldn't just leave the cowboy to fend for himself.

She backed away as the big guy punched the cowboy in the gut, but the cowboy didn't even double over. If anything, his movements became so fast they were a blur. She almost choked when the other guy pushed himself off the car and staggered toward the gun lying on the ground. Frantically, Liv looked around for anything she could use as a weapon, but there was nothing.

Running around the front of the car, her only plan of action was to come up behind him if possible, but when she got to the rear of the car, the ugliest dog she'd ever seen was standing guard over the gun and growling at the man. That horrible noise earlier must have come from this creature, and if that was the case, she would never publicly refer to him as ugly, because he'd helped save her life.

A hysterical laugh caught in her throat, and she choked it down. Sheer terror was making her think of the oddest things, but she had to focus. She must get that gun before Mr. Kale's goon did. Avoiding eye contact with the bruiser, Liv focused on the dog and inched closer, careful to stay out of reach of the guy.

"Good doggie. Very good doggie. May I come closer?" she asked in a soft tone.

The animal looked at her, then swung his head, ears flopping, back at her previous abductor and made up his mind. He padded toward the man with a low, mean growl and forced him to move backward. Liv crept toward the gun and picked it up with trembling hands. Forcing herself to take a deep breath, she gripped the pistol, calmed herself and pointed the gun at the man.

"You and your friend need to leave."

An ugly sneer marred an already unattractive face. "I'm betting you don't even know how to use that weapon. You're a city girl and don't have the guts to shoot me."

The man's words triggered her temper, especially

now that she had the upper hand. As Grandpa used to say, she was spittin' mad. "Well, now," Liv said, repeating the cowboy's words, "let's see if that's the case." She sighted the pistol and aimed it at the guy's feet. She pulled the trigger, and the bullet ricocheted off the pavement an inch from his big loafer.

His widening eyes brought a moment of satisfaction, but it didn't last long. The cowboy must have come around the car, because before she realized what was happening, he snatched the pistol out of her hand and pointed it at the bruiser.

"Do you have a cell phone?" he asked her. His words were clipped. The lazy drawl had completely disappeared. His actions and tone set off her temper once again, something her granddaddy always said would one day land her in trouble. She was normally cool, calm and collected, but after everything that had happened, her reserve was running on empty. She couldn't believe Mr. Kale's goons had caught up with her in Texas. They must have used his private jet.

Piercing the cowboy with a sharp glance, her eyes widened when an invisible fist punched her in the gut. When he'd approached earlier, she'd been terrified out of her mind, thinking she was going to die, and hadn't paid much attention, but now...

The cowboy was definitely what her sister would call a looker. His warm brown eyes were the only soft thing about him. A clean-shaven face enhanced a chiseled jaw, and his short hair—the part sticking out from beneath the cowboy hat—reminded her of dark chocolate. He was much taller than her five and a half feet, maybe six-three or more, and he had the muscular build of a man who lived and worked on the range, which she supposed he did.

Liv sharply reminded herself she'd been attracted to men before, but she didn't date because nothing was going to stand in the way of her ten-year career plan. She needed to get rid of the goons and the cowboy and get to the ranch so she could figure out how to stay out of jail and save the career she'd worked so hard to achieve.

"I have a phone in my car."

He nodded. "Call the police. It'll take them a while to get out here, but these two men aren't going anywhere. I tied the other one up."

Liv's heart almost palpitated at the mention of police. If they got involved, someone would discover the planted emails, and she'd be sitting in jail right alongside Mr. Kale's two goons. She didn't move, frantically trying to come up with a believable explanation for not calling the police, but the bruiser standing in front of them smirked and opened his big mouth.

"Yes, Miss Calloway, why don't you call the police?"

Her stomach dropped when the cowboy gave her a narrow-eyed look. "Miss Calloway? Olivia Calloway?"

She straightened her shoulders and stood tall—well, as much as she could with one shoe on. She'd have to brazen it out. She was known for her gift of gab and it was time to put it to good use, along with a little misdirection. "How do you know my name?" she asked, putting as much bravado in her voice as she could manage at the moment.

A slow grin spread across his face, and she had to blink against the force of its masculine beauty.

"Well, now," he said, the slow drawl back in his voice, "it appears as if we're neighbors. I'm Mac. I'm sure you remember me and my four brothers from school."

Liv did remember the five brothers. He was one of the wild Dolan boys. Maybe she could talk herself out of this one. She needed time to prove Mr. Kale's culpability—and her own innocence—in the murder of Mr. Burton, and she needed a place to hide to give her that time.

She studied Mac Dolan as an interesting idea popped into her head. Should she? Yes! She should. This way she wouldn't have to put her family at risk at the ranch, but first she had to throw Mr. Kale's goons off her trail and give Mac Dolan a plausible reason for not calling the police. Now that she had the upper hand with the goons, her confidence rose. She could handle this.

"Mac, it's good to see you again," she said, even though she barely remembered him. They definitely hadn't run in the same social group during their school days. She glanced at the goon, then back at Mac. "There's, uh, been a terrible misunderstanding. We don't need to call the authorities. It would be best if these two men just went along their own way." She glared at the man in front of them. "Isn't that right?"

"That's right, Miss Calloway. Just a simple misunderstanding."

Despite her newfound confidence at the turn of events, Liv shivered at the promise of retaliation shimmering in the man's eyes. She held her breath as Mac almost lazily glanced between the two of them, then lowered his rifle an inch.

"Then I suggest you untie your buddy and get out of here while you have the chance," Mac said, his words coming out slowly.

Liv released the breath she was holding and silently patted herself on the back. Everything would be okay. She just needed a safe place to hide until she figured out what to do, and Mac didn't know it yet, but he was going to help her.

Miss Calloway might look dainty, with her highlighted dirty-blond hair pulled back in a ponytail and big brown eyes chock-full of intelligence, but the woman was up to something. He would know soon enough if she was as innocent as she appeared or guilty of a crime that would land her in jail for a long time, and he'd love to get it done before Easter. All he had to do was figure out a way to stay close to her.

Mac kept an eye on the two men as one untied the other and they crawled back inside their sedan and took off. As a navy pilot, he'd seen his share of bullies, and those two were a prime example of the species. Even though Olivia was presumed to be guilty of hiring someone to commit murder, Mac cringed thinking of what could have happened to her if he hadn't come along.

He stared at her delicate hand when she gripped his sleeve, then at the biggest brown eyes he'd ever seen. Eyes that could bring a man to his knees if he allowed them, but Mac would never let that happen, especially with a female attorney. His ex-wife's lawyer had even tried to get a piece of the family ranch in the divorce. Lawyers were like Barnie on a raccoon scent or a search and rescue mission—they never gave up. And besides that, he'd never again fall for a career woman who didn't want kids. The FBI brief he'd read on Miss Calloway showed her to be a career woman right down to the toes of her—well, her one expensive shoe.

"Mac, if I may call you that. I appreciate all your help with that unfortunate situation." She released his sleeve and waved a hand in the air. "The whole thing was related to work. I'm an attorney, you know, and I was coming home for some peace and quiet in order to do some research into a big case I'm working on. Those two men weren't happy about the case."

She paused and Mac almost grinned, wondering what she'd come up with and how he could make it work for him.

"Do you live at the ranch with your mom and dad? And please, call me Liv."

The question came out of nowhere, but Mac was two steps ahead of her. The lady needed a place to hide, and he assumed the two goons knew about the Calloway ranch, but he played along because this would be a perfect way to stay close to the woman.

"Sure do, but after I came home, our parents decided to do some extensive traveling. They're out of the country for a while." She looked pleased at the news.

"And if I remember correctly, you have four younger brothers?"

"Yep, but none of them live on the ranch. Right now it's just the ranch employees, me and my dog."

She paused, as if in thought. "You know, there's a lot going on at the Calloway ranch. I was wondering..."

She allowed her words to drift away, and he knew it was a lawyer ploy.

"Wondering what?"

She tapped a manicured nail on her chin. "I was wondering if you might rent me a room and a small office space to work in. I wouldn't have to bother my family, whom I wouldn't have time to visit with much anyway. I'll just see them before I go back to the city. I work in New York, by the way."

"I'd heard through the grapevine that you were a big-city lawyer." He didn't say anything for a moment, attempting to appear as if he was mulling it over, while inside he was shouting *Yes*. Before he could answer, that earsplitting yipping came from her car again, and Liv's eyes rounded.

"Oh no, I forgot about Misty. She must be terrified."

Barnie ambled over when Liv limped quickly toward her damaged car. He had to give the woman credit. She had grit and audacity, asking to stay at his ranch, but nothing was enough to overcome the fact that she was a career woman and a possible murderer to boot.

Mac's eyes widened when she lifted a dog that resembled a long-haired rat out of the car, hugged it to her chest and rained kisses all over the animal's face. The thing had to weigh less than ten pounds. It was white with a black face except for a white spot on the end of its nose, and the ears were pointy. But that wasn't the worst part. The poor creature was dressed in the tackiest dog outfit Mac had ever seen. Where he came from, people didn't dress their dogs. Another strike against Miss Calloway. She and Mac were complete opposites—not that it really mattered.

"Well, Barnie, can you put up with that for a couple of weeks?" he whispered to his dog as he nodded toward hers. Bernie bayed softly this time. "I'll take that as a yes," Mac whispered when Liv approached with her dog in her arms, a smile pasted on her porcelain face.

"I'd like to introduce Misty. She's a highly bred papillon." She glanced at Barnie. "I assume that's your dog?"

Mac rocked back on his heels and studied her. He'd been bored for a while now, which was why he'd subcontracted this case for the FBI, but things were starting to get interesting.

"He sure is. This is Barnie. He's a highly bred bluetick coonhound and is officially certified as a search and rescue dog," he said, mimicking her uppityness. "We do a lot of hunting when we're not on a search and rescue mission."

It tickled him when she swallowed hard. "You, uh, hunt raccoons?"

"Sure do." He could tell she couldn't bring herself to ask what happened to the raccoons when they caught them, so he put her out of her misery. "I taught Barnie to track 'em, but he corners them, then we walk away and let 'em go."

She blew out a breath, and he almost grinned when she straightened her shoulders. "I grew up on our ranch, and I visit periodically, but basically I've been away a long time—first in school, then at my current position for four years."

He didn't say anything, curious to see what she would do next. It wasn't very gentlemanly, and his mother would scold him, but he couldn't stop himself.

She lifted a cute, sharp chin in the air. "Well, if you're willing to rent me some space, we should see if our dogs can get along." She eyed Barnie, and Mac imagined her brain working overtime. His dog weighed about seventy-five pounds and would squish her toy dog if he accidentally lay on her. He assumed the animal was female based on the name.

"Is he friendly?"

Mac nodded, and Liv slowly placed her trembling dog on the ground. Barnie sat on his rump and allowed the prissy dog to sniff all around him before licking Misty on the face. At first the small dog looked startled, but then she lifted her fluffy tail and marched back to Liv, only to be picked up and smothered against Liv's chest once again.

Liv gave him a weak smile, and Mac didn't doubt she was terrified on behalf of her dog, but when someone needed a place to hide, things were different.

"Okay," he said.

Her head snapped up. "Okay, what?"

"Looks like they get along, so you can stay at my place for whatever time you need." He almost felt bad at the relief that crossed her face but reminded himself of the FBI brief he'd read. If what they suspected was true, he might have just invited a killer into his home.

THREE

Liv took a deep, relieved breath and didn't question Mac allowing her to stay at his ranch. She'd flown from New York into the Midland/Odessa airport and rented a car, driving the 162 miles to Brewster County. She hadn't slept on the plane, worrying about Mr. Kale and his goons—rightly so, as it turned out.

"Will your car start?"

"What?" It took a moment to understand the simple question. She desperately needed a bath, food and sleep, most of all. The last time she checked before she was forced off the road, it was nearing noon. "Oh, I don't know. It stalled out when I, uh, ran off the road."

"I'll check it out. If we can't get it started, I'll have someone tow it to the ranch."

Liv nodded mutely and watched as Mac took long, ambling strides over to her car. That unwanted attraction pricked her heart again, and she had to remind herself once more not only of her career plans, but the fact that she would never end up living on a ranch in Texas.

He folded himself into the vehicle, and it turned over once, then the engine caught.

Liv blew out a relieved breath. At least she would have her own transportation at his ranch. She'd deal with the insurance later, although she'd probably have to pay for the damage herself, since she didn't want to call the police.

She hugged Misty closer, the thought of everything she had to deal with sitting on her shoulders like hundred-pound weights. Her dog licked her chin and she felt like wailing, but she refused to allow herself a moment of self-pity. She was a big girl and could handle anything. If she wanted to work at the Department of Justice eventually, she had to be tough.

Her pep talk worked until Mac, whom she hadn't even heard approach, lifted her chin with one callused finger and stared sympathetically into her eyes. One fat tear tracked down her cheek, and she held Misty with one arm while she swiped it away. Mac's arm fell away, and he rocked back on his heels.

"I assume you know the way since you grew up here, so I'll follow you to my ranch in case you have any car problems. That's if you're sure you don't want to go to your ranch."

Shoving away the desire to run to the bosom of her family, sleep in her childhood bed, pull the covers over her head and wish this whole mess away, she lifted her chin. "Absolutely not. I'll visit with them later, after I get my work caught up." She stared into those warm brown eyes, hoping she sounded strong, while inside she was quivering with doubt, but she knew this was the best thing to do. Mac could handle whatever came her way, and she wasn't quite ready to involve her family in this mess until she had a better understanding of what was happening. She'd been headed home, but since this opportunity arose, it was the better option.

He touched the edge of his cowboy hat and gave a half nod, and she limped on one shoe to her car. Mac had left the driver's door open, and she spotted her other shoe on the floorboard. The memory of it slipping off when those goons grabbed her out of her car made her shiver, but she grabbed her shoe, slipped the heel back on her foot and situated Misty in the safety carrier sitting in the passenger seat before slipping in and putting the car in Drive. She pulled out and got in front of Mac, who was sitting in his truck waiting to follow her.

They were only about five miles from his ranch, and soon she was pulling onto a beautiful paved driveway lined with trees. She'd been by here several times when she was in school, but it looked like a completely different place. When the house came into view, her breath caught. It no longer resembled the old ranch house that used to be there. It was absolutely gorgeous, a large white classical ranch house with a wide, wraparound porch. Something to the far left caught her attention, and her eyes widened.

A huge, gleaming white airplane sat in the middle of a dirt airstrip, and she wondered if that was the plane her sister had been attacked in when fighting an unknown enemy who turned out to be their neighbor's wife. The woman was aware of the shell oil hidden on the Calloway property and was willing to kill to obtain it. Tempe knew Mac better than Olivia, because they'd both been in the Blue Angels while in the navy.

She peered at the house again. When she was in school the Dolans weren't exactly poor, but they hadn't had money like this. She briefly wondered what had happened to change their circumstances. Cattle prices hadn't risen that much in the intervening years. But how they achieved their success wasn't important right now and really none of her business.

She put her car in Park and looked at Misty. "Well, girl, is this a bad idea? We can always turn around and go stay with Tempe. I'm sure Kylo will be nicer to you than last time. Tempe's been training him."

Misty gave one short, disgruntled bark.

Liv gripped the steering wheel as she watched Mac and his dog exit the old truck. "Okay, we'll see how this works out, and if we're not comfortable, we'll go to the Calloway ranch."

Even though it would be relatively safe at her family's ranch, it'd be better here. She'd let Tempe know what was going on so the family could take precautions, just in case, but hopefully, without Liv there, Mr. Kale wouldn't risk exposing himself to more scrutiny by attacking anyone at the Calloway ranch.

She paused, her mind outpacing her exhaustion for a moment. But the one question she couldn't figure was why Mac would agree to let her stay at his ranch. It didn't appear as if his family needed the rent money. With no time to ponder it more—because really, what choice did she have?—Liv took a deep breath and opened her door.

The familiar smells of hay and livestock hit her with the force of the past, and she realized she'd missed this, even though when she left for school, she hadn't thought she'd ever appreciate the smells of ranch life again. Sometimes time and distance changed things.

Mac coming toward her car cut her memories short, and she started doing what she did best—talking.

"Mac, what a beautiful place your family has turned this into. I certainly appreciate the offer of a room and office. We'll be out of your hair before Easter." She reached inside the car and pulled Misty from her car seat, effectively placing a barrier between her and the most handsome, rugged man she'd been around in years. Her heart thumped against her chest, but she attributed it to everything she'd been through over the last twenty-four hours, not the man staring at her and Misty as if they'd beamed down from another planet. She needed to get settled before she fell flat on her face from exhaustion.

"As I said, I'm happy to compensate you for an office, room and board."

He smiled, and the right side of his mouth hitched up farther than the left, making her traitorous heart beat faster than it should under the circumstances. It was only fatigue combined with everything she'd been through, she reminded herself.

"No need to worry about that. We have plenty of room, and that's what neighbors are for. Pop your trunk and I'll grab your luggage."

His assurance that she didn't need to pay rent gave her pause. Was he really just that neighborly, or was something else going on? But at the moment, she had few options and chose to ignore her gut warning. Regardless of his reasons, she'd insist he take the money before she headed back to New York.

Liv hit the trunk button on her key fob and followed him to the back of the car, cringing when she passed the dented passenger side. If it wasn't for Mac, she could very well be dead right now. She cringed again when he stood staring at the two huge suitcases stuffed inside the trunk. Not wanting him to think she'd packed all that stuff for herself, she quickly explained.

"The one on the right is mine, and the other belongs to Misty."

His incredulous expression rubbed her the wrong way, and the first thought that popped into her head came out of her mouth. "Is that a problem?" She tried to shove him out of the way and grab the handle of one suitcase, but a large, callused hand wrangled it away from her.

"None at all, Miss Calloway, none at all."

"I told you to call me Liv." She stepped back, embarrassed, but she shouldn't be. She'd only packed the essentials for both her and Misty. Even though it was warmer in Texas, her dog was easily chilled.

She jumped when something cool touched her leg. But it was just Mac's highly bred bluetick coonhound. Barnie wore an expression identical to his owner, as if Liv and Misty had beamed down from another planet.

"Come on," Mac said as he took long strides toward the wide front porch steps. "Patsy probably has lunch on the table. We can eat, then we'll get you settled in."

Misty whined when Liv tightened her arms around the small dog, and she immediately loosened them. Who was Patsy? Was Mac married? She hadn't even thought about that until this very moment. She couldn't stay here if he had a wife and children. That would place them in the same danger she was trying to protect her family from.

But as she crossed the threshold from the porch to the house and into a foyer decorated in a Western theme, the biggest question plaguing her mind was why Mac had so easily agreed to allow her and Misty to stay here.

The two suitcases Mac carried into the house felt like they weighed a ton. How much luggage could one woman and a dog need, even for a lengthy stay? He placed the suitcases on the floor of the foyer and turned to find Patsy had stepped out of the kitchen, wiping her hands on a towel. Patsy was really the force behind the ranch, feeding the ranch hands and making sure the house ran properly, especially with his parents gone on an extended vacation. She'd been with them since he and his brothers were small boys and considered herself part of the family, which she was.

He didn't like the initial gleam in her eye when she first noticed Liv and Misty, which quickly turned to astonishment as she assessed them more closely. Liv's business suit appeared as if she'd slept in it and the dog was dressed in a spiffy outfit, but the main thing was that they both still reeked of sophistication and were completely out of place on a ranch.

Patsy had been after Mac to start dating, claiming two years was long enough to get over the shark he had divorced, but he grinned inside when their longtime cook turned her shocked gaze on him. Liv was representative of what he'd spent a lot of time and money getting away from, but just to make sure Patsy didn't get any matchmaking ideas in her head, he said, "Patsy, this is Liv Calloway. She owns part of the Calloway ranch. I happened upon her on the way home, and she's asked to rent a room and office for a short time to catch up on some of her lawyer work, since it's so busy at her place. It's pretty quiet here until Easter, so I told her to make herself at home. She can use Mom's small office to do her work."

He rocked back on his heels and grinned when Patsy stared at him as if he was a stranger, but he straightened back up real quick when a challenging spark lit her eyes and she turned on the charm for Liv.

"Liv, yes, you're one of the Calloway girls, and what a cute dog you've got there." Outfitted in worn jeans and a faded plaid shirt, Patsy stepped forward and took Liv by the elbow, leading her toward the kitchen. "C'mon, you look like a feather could blow you over, you're so thin. Let's get some food in your belly and we'll get your sweet pup some water, then we'll get you settled in."

Liv peered helplessly over her shoulder, but Mac just shrugged. Patsy was a force to be reckoned with and one tough cookie. She had to be, practically helping his mother raise five rowdy boys. He lingered in the foyer a moment, wondering if Liv was innocent or guilty of the information in the FBI dossier. She looked so petite and fragile. She couldn't be over five and a half feet tall, but that didn't mean she couldn't hire a hit man to commit murder. He grinned again when he thought of her perfect aim with her assailant's pistol. But his grin slid away when he remembered the life-threatening situation she was in.

His chin jerked up and his gut filled with dread when the ladies' laughter filtered through the open arch leading to the kitchen. He quickly made his way into the inviting, homey room. The last thing he needed was for Liv and Patsy to become bosom buddies, because never in a million years was he getting married again, no matter what Patsy said or did, and she'd better not set her sights on Liv.

He came to an abrupt halt when the domestic scene in the kitchen hit him like a fist to the gut. Liv had tied one of Patsy's old aprons around her waist and kicked off her high heels and was now helping put lunch on the table in the kitchen he'd renovated. With the maple wood paneling, hardwood floors and pot-bellied stove creating a comfortable warmth around her, Liv looked as if she belonged there, in his world.

Misty moved close enough to sniff Barnie, and Mac's highly trained coonhound raised his head from his dog bed in the corner and licked the little dog on the face. The sappy look on Barnie's face reminded Mac of what he probably looked like the first time he saw Liv on the side of the road, and it didn't sit well with him.

He sternly reminded himself of all the things standing between them. She was a career woman, and he wanted a family, if—and it was a big if—he ever found the right woman. She was an attorney, and after dealing with his ex-wife's lawyer, he would never tie himself to a woman in that profession. She lived in the city and he planned to live the rest of his life on the ranch. And most importantly, she was in the middle of an ongoing FBI investigation.

Having gotten his head back on straight, his shoulders relaxed, and he ambled into the kitchen and pulled out a chair at the large, solid oak table. They had a fancy dining room, but for the most part the family tended to eat in the kitchen. The ranch hands ate their dinner in the bunkhouse.

The women quit chatting and took their seats. His stomach rumbled when the sweet smells of meat loaf and mashed potatoes wafted upward. Just as he was getting ready to say grace, Liv scooted her chair back and Misty jumped into her lap.

Mac's incredulous expression didn't go over well.

"Is there a problem?" she asked, her chin raised in challenge.

A retort formed in his mind, but before he spoke, he noticed the blue bruising under her eyes, revealing her exhaustion.

"Nope, none at all," he said. His mama had raised him to be a gentleman—well, she'd done the best she could with five wild heathens underfoot. He nodded at Patsy, said grace and started shoveling meat loaf into his mouth. He watched with interest as Liv fed delicate, tiny morsels of food to her dog while she ate.

The dossier he'd read had given him basic information on Olivia Calloway, but Mac needed to know more in order to dig out the truth. He needed to know what made Liv tick. Who were her friends? His fork stopped halfway to his mouth. Did she have a boyfriend? The dossier stated she'd never been married, but was she seriously involved with someone? His gut rebelled at the idea but soon eased. If there was a boyfriend in the picture, she would likely be with him instead of hiding out at Mac's ranch. He tuned back into the conversation between the two women when his name was mentioned.

"Yes, Mac rebuilt the house for his parents and repaired a lot of things on the ranch, too," Patsy was saying. Mac wanted to zip Patsy's mouth shut when Liv glanced at him with a calculating look in her eye. The same look he'd seen on his ex-wife's face when she learned he wasn't just an old cowpoke. He shot Patsy a *be quiet* look and graced Liv with a lazy grin.

"And he's also…" Patsy trailed off when she finally got the message.

He leaned back in his chair and rubbed his stomach. "Yeah, my brothers and I all pitched in and helped, and we decided our parents deserved a long vacation after raising all us boys."

Liv glanced between him and Patsy, and he knew when her exhaustion overcame her curiosity. She placed her napkin on the table just so.

"Patsy," she said, "thank you for the wonderful lunch. Can I help you clean up?"

Patsy scooted her chair back and pushed herself to her feet. "Nope, let's get you settled in. I suggest you and that precious baby of yours take yourselves a little nap."

Liv smiled tightly at Mac. "I appreciate you letting me stay here so I can catch up on my work. I'm not a guest, and I insist on paying, so go on about your business. You won't even know I'm here."

A ringing phone preempted Mac's response, and he watched Liv pull a cell phone out of her skirt pocket. She sighed and took the call.

"Babette, I was getting ready to call you, but this is not a good time." Mac heard a strong, loud voice on the other end of the line.

"Where are you? I know you're not at home, because I just stopped by your place."

Liv turned away, and Mac couldn't hear any more. He pushed himself away from the table but froze half-way out of his seat when a loud boom shook the house's foundation beneath his feet, shattering the peace he'd fought so hard to find after the failure of his disastrous marriage.

FOUR

Liv dropped the phone she was holding, and her frantic gaze shot straight to Mac. Had Mr. Kale's goons followed them to the ranch to destroy Mac's family property? Babette's hysterical shrieks rose from the phone lying on the floor, and she picked it up with trembling fingers.

"Babette, I'll call you later," she whispered. She punched the phone off with her best friend still screaming, wanting to know what that loud noise was.

Mac was already out of his chair and headed out the door. Liv plopped Misty onto Barnie's dog bed. "Barnie, you take care of my baby," she whispered, her heart in her throat. Patsy was staring out the kitchen window, a stricken look on her face.

Liv didn't bother to look out the window but hurried after Mac, feet still bare, to see what danger she had unwittingly brought to his ranch. If anything happened to one of them, she'd never forgive herself.

When she stepped onto the porch, she stood, mesmerized by the flames devouring her rental car, and started shaking. Mac and a few ranch hands had pulled out hoses and were dousing the flames, but Liv had no doubt this was the work of Mr. Kale's goons.

A terrifying thought crossed her mind. Had they followed her here? Were they now positioned somewhere, waiting to take her out? She scanned the area around the house and barn. Maybe the men had planted a timed device on her car just in case the kidnapping failed and she was supposed to be in the vehicle when the explosion occurred.

Something whizzed by her ear, and a soft thud sounded behind her. It took her a moment to realize it was a bullet, and just as she jerked her body out of the way a second one whizzed by. Kale knew where she was! She frantically watched as Mac left the inferno blazing behind him and took the steps three at a time. Two large hands gripped her shoulders, and she stared into concerned dark brown eyes rimmed in gold. He could easily get shot in the back without even being aware of what was going on. She wasn't ready to lay her cards on the table, but she didn't want him hurt.

"Liv, are you okay? You shouldn't be out here barefoot. Let's get you back inside. The boys can handle the fire."

Liv grabbed his hand and pulled him inside. She wasn't worried about the ranch hands. Mr. Kale only wanted her dead. Additional deaths would raise more suspicion. She couldn't stop shaking, knowing how close to getting shot she'd just come, but she had to act normally until she figured out how to handle this dangerous situation.

Oh, how she was tempted to fall into Mac's strong arms and let him handle this mess, but that wasn't fair.

And then there were those incriminating emails sitting in her Sent box, just waiting to make her look guilty of murder. Liv closed her eyes and took a deep breath. She had to leave, but she couldn't go home, either. She had to find a place to hide, giving her time to find proof against her boss and his goons.

Lifting her chin, she said, "The vehicle must have had a malfunction of some sort." She couldn't control the tremble in her voice, but she plowed ahead. "I—I think it's best if Misty and I leave. I appreciate you agreeing to let me work here, but, well—" She motioned at the burning car, at a loss for words for maybe the first time in her life, and said weakly, "I think it's best if I make other arrangements."

Mac gripped her shoulders and looked her right in the eye. "Liv, if you're in any kind of trouble, maybe I can help." He waited, almost as if he knew something she didn't, as if he wanted her to confess something, but she shook off her imaginings and pulled away from his hands.

"I'll be fine. I just need a quiet place to stay for a few weeks."

He rocked back on his heels and grinned. "Well, then, looks to me like you've found the right place." He placed a hand on her shoulder and pulled her farther into the house. "Come on, let's get you settled in."

Liv skidded to a stop in her bare feet. "Mac, didn't you hear me? I think Misty and I should leave. I'll call a car rental place and have a vehicle delivered."

He pulled her into the kitchen where Patsy had evidently calmed down and was finishing the dishes. "Patsy, you tell Liv here that one little car accidentally catching on fire is no big deal, that she's welcome to stay."

Liv wondered at the questioning look Patsy gave Mac before her mouth split in a big grin and she moved forward, taking Liv's arm away from Mac. "Of course you're staying here. And look at your sweet little dog over there, all cuddled up to Barnie."

Liv jerked her gaze to the massive dog bed lying in the corner of the kitchen, and her chin dropped. Her sweet baby was curled into Barnie's big chest, and she was fast asleep. Barnie was wide-awake, and his expression practically dared anyone to disturb his new charge.

"See there," Mac chimed in, "your dog looks happy as a bug in a rug."

Liv remembered the way Mac had handled the goons and made up her mind to stay, because really, where else did she have to go? In school the Dolan boys were known to be rough and rowdy and affectionately known as troublemakers by the teachers, due to their charming ability to talk themselves out of any corner they found themselves in. Mac had grown up tough. He could handle it if anything dangerous occurred.

She smiled, even though she felt like screaming at the world. She'd worked so hard to get where she was, and her corrupt boss could ruin years' worth of hard work—plus there was the possibility of jail time if she couldn't find the proof to clear her name. "Misty does look happy. Patsy, if you wouldn't mind showing me my office and room, I think I will lie down for a little while."

She felt like collapsing, but she still had to call Babette before she could rest, and she dreaded that conversation. Leaving Misty sleeping under Barnie's protective watch after Patsy promised to bring her up when she woke, Liv followed the housekeeper up a beautiful curved stairwell with railings made of some type of satiny dark wood and to a room down the hall.

"Oh, it's lovely," she breathed, following Patsy into the bedroom. Light floral curtains practically floated from the ceiling to the hardwood floor, and the matching comforter showcased a gorgeous headboard carved with a forest scene of deer and other wildlife. It appeared to have been done by hand and must have cost a fortune.

Patsy rubbed a hand down her plaid shirt while staring longingly at Liv's wrinkled but feminine business suit. Liv briefly wondered what that was all about, but she was too tired to think. Mac came in behind them with both suitcases in tow. He nodded at the women before disappearing back out the door.

"The bathroom is through there—" Patsy waved a hand toward the only other door in the room "—and Mac's mom's office is the next door down the hall right beside this bedroom. Just yell if you need anything."

"Thank you, Patsy, for being so kind," Liv said with the last of her reserve. Patsy nodded and closed the door behind her when she left the room. Sitting on the side of the bed, Liv fell backward onto the soft mattress and closed her eyes, wondering how her life had spun so far out of control in such a short amount of time.

It was amazing that Mac had been the one to find her fighting those goons. In the safety of this room, with time to think, she was sure she would have found a way out of the situation, but the memory of those men manhandling her had her shivering again.

Her phone notified her of an incoming call, and she blew out a breath while digging it back out of her pocket. "Hey, Babette," she said, then waited for the explosion, which didn't take but a split second.

"Liv, you better tell me what's going on, because you're not at home and you're always either at work or at home on Friday and Saturday nights because you *never date*! You're so fired up about your ten-year career plan and all those crusty old lawyers you work for, you're missing everything life has to offer. And what's with that loud noise I heard? Is Misty okay? What's going on?"

For the first time since leaving Mr. Kale's office the evening before, Liv smiled. Babette was the only person Liv knew who could outtalk her. The woman was a babbling brook when she got riled.

"Misty's fine, but, well…" Liv closed her eyes, and a tear tracked down her cheek.

"You're crying, aren't you? Did one of those morons you work for upset you? You tell me what happened and I'll pay the uppity man a personal visit."

And that's why Liv loved Babette to pieces. She was always in her friend's corner no matter what. "You could say that they upset me," Liv whispered.

Liv wasn't surprised when Babette quickly picked up on the fact that this was much more than the usual office antics. "Liv, tell me what's happening."

Liv started at the beginning and filled her best friend in on everything, including Mac's rescue, all the way to her car exploding.

"Those rats. I never did like those guys you work for, especially Kale Jr." Babette's response didn't surprise her, considering her friend's background. She paused, then said, "Liv, this is dangerous business. Your life is at risk." She took a deep breath. "I'm coming out there."

Before Liv could protest, the line went dead. Instead of calling her friend back, she pulled the comforter from the end of the bed and covered herself up. She was asleep in seconds.

Mac squirmed under Patsy's wrathful gaze down in the kitchen. "I changed your diapers, Mac Dolan, and I know when you're up to something." She pointed a finger at the ceiling. "Something that involves that poor girl, and I want to know what it is this minute or I'm calling your mother."

"Now, Patsy—"

She cut him off at the quick. "Don't you 'now' me. I also know you contract out with the FBI, so start talking or I'm picking up the phone."

Mac blew out a long breath. He was smart enough to know when he was licked. "Listen, Patsy, you know I can't reveal FBI information, but yes, Olivia Calloway could be in a great deal of trouble if what they suspect proves to be true."

Patsy stepped closer and got in his face. "I knew Liv and Tempe's granddaddy, and I knew their parents before they died in that plane crash when those girls were teenagers. They've recently come into money after finding that oil on their property, but both of them fought hard to make something of themselves." She poked him in the chest. "You just do whatever it is you do and prove that girl innocent."

Mac could see where this was leading. "And what if I find out she's guilty, Patsy?" He closed his eyes, prayed for patience, then opened them again. "And I know what you're thinking. I'm not anywhere near ready to get involved with a woman." He added gently, "She's just like my ex-wife. Based on the information I've been privy to so far, it appears her career is the most important thing in the world to her, and she may even be a criminal. Please, please stay out of this and let me find out what's going on."

A sad look crossed her face, but then she straightened her shoulders and a twinkle lit her eyes. "All right, Mac, you go right ahead and do what you have to, but I'm in that girl's corner."

He gave up, pushed himself away from the table and stood. "Understood." And he did understand, he thought as he made his way to the smoldering car.

Boone, his ranch foreman, nodded at him while aiming a water hose at the hot vehicle. Mac asked to borrow a working glove and slipped it on his hand before crouching down and peering under the car. A bomb with a timer would be the logical choice. The men must have slipped it on the car before he got there as a backup, in case things didn't go as planned, or to destroy the evidence of a struggle.

He immediately spotted remnants of the small device underneath the car, but he found something else much more disturbing. With his gloved hand, he plucked the small tracking device placed well away from the bomb, probably another backup in case Liv managed to get away from them.

But as soon as the tracking device pulled free, another device started blinking red. "Boone, run! Get away from the car," he yelled while scrambling out from underneath the vehicle as fast as he could.

Instead of listening, Boone grabbed him and helped him get clear of the car before the second bomb detonated. It was much smaller than the first one and only made a minor noise, but it had him wiping the moisture from his eyes, which stung from the smoke. When his vision cleared, he stared at what was left of the vehicle, which was next to nothing.

"You okay, boss?" his unflappable ranch foreman asked.

"Yeah. Listen, I want you and the other guys to be on alert for any strangers poking around or anything that looks odd or out of place."

Boone grinned, and six decades' worth of sun-leathered skin wrinkled his face. "You want us to help you watch out for that little lady you brought home with you, too?"

The foreman was nobody's fool. Mac had always thought common sense more valuable than a big degree any day of the week. "Yeah, I'd appreciate that. She might have grown up in Texas, but she's been in the city too long. I doubt she remembers what it's like to live on a ranch."

"You got it. Let me know if you need anything else. The boys and I'll get this cleaned up—unless you want to call the law?"

He appreciated that Boone didn't ask too many questions about why Liv was there, but Mac's foreman never intruded into someone's privacy.

Mac shook his head, and Boone touched the brim of his hat and disappeared into the barn. Heading toward the house, Mac decided not to mention the second explosion and the tracking device to Liv, because she hadn't leveled with him yet.

It was time to do a little searching of his own. Once inside, he approached a door at the end of the hall and punched a code into the pad on the wall allowing him entrance. He made sure the door closed securely before hitting the light switch on the wall.

He took the stairs two at a time, leading to the basement. This setup was just temporary, but it worked for him. He'd move his private office from his parents' house to his own home on a prime spot on the ranch once he completed construction. It would be nice to find some peace and quiet in a place he could truly call his own.

Relaxing into the ergonomic office chair, he hit a button that turned on all the screens sitting in a semicircle on his desk and booted up multiple computers that he used in his main job as a financial planner for wealthy clients. He needed to know more about Kale, Kale & Johnston and get a bead on those two goons.

Due to his financial planning, his contracted work with the FBI and the contacts he'd made while in the military, he knew a lot of people around the globe. Some of them revealed their faces and real names, and others chose to stay anonymous, only offering a cyber name and a way to get in touch.

Mac's fingers hovered above the keyboard, and a

spike of adrenaline surged through his system. Being an adrenaline junkie was one reason he'd been such a hotshot Blue Angel pilot, but he'd seen men die young due to that particular lifestyle, and he'd grown up, especially after his divorce. He took a calming breath and started typing. It didn't take long to put the word out that he wanted the scuttlebutt on Kale, Kale & Johnston and the big man's goons and was willing to pay if the information was reliable. The money would come out of his own pocket. He didn't care to share his contacts with the FBI.

While he was there, he checked on several investments he'd recommended for some of his clients. His system was simple and used good old common sense. His recommendations were based on things people wanted or needed.

While waiting, he ran a regular search on Olivia Calloway and came up with a few hits. Her full name was Olivia Shannon Calloway, and he whistled when he noted her credentials. She'd gone to Harvard, finished one year early, then easily got into their law program. She had been working for Kale, Kale & Johnston since graduation.

He frowned. Why would someone as smart as Liv be foolish enough to send an email from her work account to a hit man requesting a job, as the FBI dossier claimed? An email that could be found even if deleted. Before he could ponder that thought, his computer dinged, and his gaze flew to his main screen. He tapped a button and placed a tracer on the incoming email but quickly realized it wouldn't do any good.

The email was from someone calling themselves Spider, and he'd never been able to trace the guy. Or girl. He'd dealt with them before and the information they'd shared had always been reliable, so he paid close attention. He scanned the data and frowned. Spider recommended Mac steer clear of Olivia's law firm, claiming they were bad news, in a deadly way. The first email disappeared minutes after Mac opened it, and a second one popped up. Mac grinned when he read the names of the two goons who had tried to kidnap Liv, with an added warning to be careful. Then it, too, quickly disappeared. The names resounded in his head. Tommy and Gordon Genovese.

"Gotcha," Mac said out loud. Now to find the two men.

FIVE

Liv woke to a sweet doggie kiss on her chin and the wondrous smells of coffee, bacon and probably all the trimmings of a nice, fattening ranch-style breakfast, reminding her once again of her roots. Her stomach rumbled, and she gave Misty a big smooch before sitting up and throwing off the comforter she'd covered herself with. She stared at her mussed-up dog and raised a hand to the rat's nest sitting on top of her own head. She couldn't believe she'd slept the whole afternoon and the night through.

Laughing out loud, she hugged her dog to her chest. "If Babette were here, she'd have me in a hair salon and you in her dog salon so fast it'd make our heads spin." Misty gave her a doggie grin. "I doubt Mac would consider us very attractive right now, my friend." She blew out a breath. "Not that it really matters. He might be a looker, as Babette would say, but we have absolutely nothing in common." Misty gazed up at her with adoring eyes, and Liv snorted. "Don't get any ideas about Barnie, because the minute I have evidence proving my innocence, we're out of here."

Misty sniffed, and Liv pushed herself off the bed. Rummaging around in her suitcase, she pulled out a pair of worn jeans and a faded Western shirt, remnants of her past that she'd shoved into the back of her closet in New York. She kept them available for when she visited her sister, aunt and niece at the family ranch. She stared at the worn cowboy boots she lifted out next and sighed heavily. The clothes were comfortable, but even though she'd been having nostalgic feelings, she just wasn't into ranch life.

She loved nice clothes, the theater, upscale restaurants and even the smell of the city. The one thing she didn't like was a back-stabbing boss who set her up to take the fall for a crime she didn't commit. The enormity of her situation threatened to swamp her, but she forced her shoulders back and marched to the bathroom. There *was* one thing about growing up on a ranch that stuck with her. Her granddaddy had taught her no matter how many times the other guy knocked you down, you came up swinging. She would clear her name and get back on track with her career plan.

As soon as she saw her reflection in the mirror, she recoiled in horror. Her expensively highlighted dirty-blond hair was a tangled mess. Her makeup was smudged all over her face, and her beautiful business suit—which she'd slept in—was wrinkled beyond repair.

Liv closed her eyes in mortification when she heard heavy footsteps coming down the upstairs corridor toward her room. She stepped out of the bathroom just as Mac, or she assumed it was Mac, knocked on the door. She was a mess, but there was nothing she could do about it. "Come in."

He scanned the room when he entered, and then his eyes shifted to her. She lifted her chin in defiance of her appearance. He was the one knocking on her door first thing in the morning.

"I just came to tell you breakfast will be on the table soon." He studied her closer. "Are you okay? You look a little peaked."

Embarrassment almost got the best of her, but she mumbled, "I went to the bathroom and, um, got a shock when I looked in the mirror." She ran a hand over her tangled hair, and he just stood there, staring at her.

That didn't sit well, and her chin shot up. She might not be at her best at the moment, but that was no reason to stare. "Misty and I will be down shortly. Thank you for letting me know about breakfast."

His gaze drifted toward her bedraggled dog, then he shrugged and left the room. Liv took a deep breath. She really should be grateful. Mac was allowing her to stay in his home, allowing her time to get her chaotic life under control.

Grabbing her clothes, she went to the bathroom, grabbed a quick shower, dressed herself and Misty and headed downstairs. Her stomach rumbled again.

Liv stopped short and almost swallowed her tongue when she crossed the threshold of the kitchen. Patsy and Mac sat at the table, but it was the two men standing at the kitchen counter that arrested her attention. One was pouring himself a cup of coffee, and the other one gave her a hard look.

The one pouring the coffee was absolutely stunning—she'd almost describe him as pretty. His face was flawless, and the sun pouring through the kitchen window not only highlighted his blond hair but warmed the golden tones of his skin. He wore pressed jeans and a starched shirt. The other guy was huge, bald-headed and looked like he belonged in a motorcycle gang. Misty squirmed in her arms about the same time Mac snorted.

"He has that effect on everyone," he said with a touch of humor and waved a hand in the air. "Liv, meet Rex, my next-to-youngest brother, and his friend Cal."

Liv groped for a chair, pulled it out and sat, all without taking her eyes off Rex. She ignored the other man, who reminded her way too much of Mr. Kale's goons. "You're, ah, Mac's brother?"

Mac sighed heavily, causing her to tear her gaze away from Rex. Liv realized that although Rex might be gorgeous, Mac won hands down in the looks department with his rugged appearance.

"Rex is the only one of us boys who took after our mother. The rest of us are the spitting image of Dad."

"Cute dog you have there," the dazzling man said, but Liv's eyes were glued on Mac, and she didn't appreciate the disbelief written all over his face.

"What?" she demanded.

"You look different, is all," Mac said with a heavy Texas twang, "with the Western attire instead of the business suit." He pointed at Misty. "Your dog, too, with her, ah, matching outfit."

Liv looked down at her jeans, Western shirt and scuffed boots, then checked the matching outfit Babette had made for Misty's forays to Texas. The clothes were perfectly acceptable, and she chose to ignore Mac's comment when Patsy placed a plate piled high with food in front of her.

With a wide smile on her face and a twinkle in her eye, Patsy said, "Dig in. We've already eaten."

Liv barely stopped herself from leaning back when the bald guy approached and held out his arms.

"Can I hold your dog?"

She shot Mac a frantic look, but he shrugged. Rex saved the day. With a soft expression, he said, "Go ahead, Liv, Cal will be gentle."

Liv tentatively handed over her dog and stared at the transformation on Cal's face. He smiled, revealing two gold teeth, and the jagged scar running down his left cheek didn't seem nearly so scary.

Her attention back on the plate in front of her, Liv briefly wondered what Patsy was so happy about, but her stomach growled as the combination of bacon, eggs, gravy biscuits and pork tenderloin reached her nose, and she didn't care. She breathed in the sweet aroma of a ranch breakfast and had to admit there were some things she missed. She picked up a fork and dug in, refusing to think about all the calories she'd have to work off later.

While she ate, Rex sat across from her at the table, Cal beside him cuddling Misty. She was shocked when Misty gave him a kiss on the chin. Rex's gaze swung between Liv and Mac. He had a knowing look in his eye, and she briefly wondered what that was about, but it really wasn't important.

"So, Rex, if I remember correctly, you were three years behind me in school. What have you been doing with yourself since graduation?"

His crystalline blue eyes twinkled, and Mac snorted. Liv ignored Mac and focused on Rex.

"I'm a pastor."

Her hand stopped midway to her mouth, and she saw Mac grin out of the corner of her eye. She carefully laid her fork down. "Well, that's nice." She cleared her throat, because, well, this was uncomfortable, especially since she'd given up on God a long time ago when He'd taken her parents from her. "Are you the pastor of a local church?" she asked, more to be polite than anything else.

Rex smiled, and the sun filling the kitchen seemed even brighter. "I'm a pastor at the state penitentiary." He waved a hand toward the large man holding Misty. "Cal is having a bit of a hard time at the moment, and Mac has agreed to let him stay here for a little while until he can get back on his feet." He leaned forward with a gleam in his eye and braced both elbows on the table. "And what brings you to the Dolan ranch?"

Liv was glad when Patsy slapped Rex on the hand with a spatula. "Mind your manners, young man, and quit being nosy."

Liv's gift of gab went on sabbatical. "Well, I'm glad you're in a profession you appear to enjoy," she said weakly instead of answering his question.

Everyone sitting at the table tensed when Barnie hopped out of his dog bed and bayed loud enough to burst her eardrums. Mere seconds later, an alarm pierced the air, and before Liv could blink, Mac and his brother disappeared.

The ranch's perimeter security had been breached. Mac jumped up from the table and headed straight for his computer room with Rex hot on his heels. He knew Patsy would delay Liv and take care of her and Cal while he found out what had tripped the ranch's elaborate alarm system.

After seeing a lot of terrible things in the military, and after choosing to contract out with the FBI, he had invested in a state-of-the-art security system, then tinkered with it to suit his purposes. He wanted his family fully protected at all costs.

Punching in the code, he swept through the door and his fingers hit his keyboard before he was even seated. Several screens lit up, and he brought up video surveillance of all the ranch's quadrants. He zeroed in on the one that was tagged and went live. When nothing appeared out of the ordinary, he replayed the last ten minutes of video.

He was aware of Rex hovering over his shoulder, but he ignored his nosy brother. Rex knew all about the security system, and he didn't need to explain what was happening. He studied the video as it replayed and pressed a key to freeze the frame when a small object came into view. After backing it up a bit, he moved it forward in slow motion. Then froze it again and sat back in his chair while he studied the object.

"What is it?" Rex asked, so close to his ear that Mac pushed his chair back, causing his brother to stumble.

"What'd ya do that for?" Rex groused, gaining his balance.

Mac whipped his chair around. "We have a serious situation here. Stay out of my way until I figure out what's going on."

Rex threw up his hands. "Fine. But I'm here to help in any way I can."

Mac softened, staring at his brother, a man who dedicated his life to helping people on a daily basis. "I appreciate it."

Rex nodded, and Mac turned back to the screen, but his brother had always been nosy and couldn't help himself. "So, what's the deal with Liv?"

Frustration ripped through Mac, but he softened when Rex sighed and said, "Look at us, acting like we're kids again." Rex paused. "Listen, Mac, the whole family knows it's none of our business, but we've been worried about you since the divorce. Then I come home and find Olivia Calloway staying here, and, well, I was hoping you'd finally moved on."

Mac concentrated on the computer screens. "I'm a little busy here, Rex," he ground out.

Rex sighed again. "I'm assuming that sweet girl has something to do with your contracted work with the FBI?"

Mac had shared his side profession with his family, just to be cautious. He wanted them to be informed in case his work ever followed him home, just as it had in Liv's case.

"You know I can't disclose anything I'm working on, but I will tell you that thing on my computer screen is a small drone, probably sent to retrieve information on our property." He swiveled back around and faced his brother. "Listen, Rex, Liv is in danger, so any time you're here at the ranch, be careful." He paused before adding, "And don't get it into that thick skull of yours that anything is going to happen between me and Liv in a personal way. Butt out of my private life." Mac gave up when Rex nodded seriously, but he had a gleam in his eye that Mac recognized only too well.

"Gotcha."

A change of subject was in order. "What's Cal's story? You've brought strays home before, but none as tough-looking as he is. Is it safe for Liv, having him in the house?"

That gleam intensified, but Mac ignored it.

"He's gentle as a lamb. He did well when he started volunteering at the animal program at the prison. He's helped a lot of inmates. But he lost his job recently. There's not enough money in the program for a salary, and the prison won't offer him a position, so I thought he could stay here and help out around the ranch awhile until he got on his feet."

Mac sighed. "You've brought other people here, and I don't mind them using the ranch until they find their way, but if he's happy helping you at the prison, why not let him stay at your place?"

Rex shrugged. "The ranch is a good, wholesome place for him until he gets a paying job. Just give him something to do on the ranch, and I'll see if I can find him something more permanent. I'll pop in and check on him." He paused. "And I appreciate the money you donated to the prison. It helped to keep my programs going."

Mac shrugged. "You do good work." He wasn't happy about having Cal under his roof when he was dealing with Liv's situation, but he'd do it. When his Goody Two-shoes brother wanted something, he had a way of piling on the guilt.

"Are you going to tell Liv about the drone?" Rex asked, bringing the conversation back to the woman sitting in his kitchen decked out in perfectly acceptable

Western attire. Mac inwardly rolled his eyes. Even her dog had on a Western outfit. But he couldn't help but remember how natural and comfortable it felt to have her sitting at his breakfast table.

"Yes, I'll tell her." Maybe it would encourage her to confide in him. If she didn't, he would have to work around that until she came clean with him—unless things became too dangerous or he proved her guilt or innocence.

Mac jerked in his chair when a security breach caused the alarm to start screeching again. His fingers flying over the keyboard, he went live on all four quadrants of the ranch, and he froze when he spotted a drone headed straight toward the house. It wasn't the drone itself that caused a ripple of fear to undulate up his back. It was what was attached underneath that raised the hair on his arms. The thing was armed with four small missiles.

He barely got out of his chair before he heard glass shatter and a terrified scream reverberate through the house.

SIX

After the first alarm went off and Mac and Rex left the room, Patsy had reassured Liv that it was probably a malfunction of some sort and nothing to worry about. But when it started screeching again, Liv sat straight up in her chair, worried. Could it be something related to her situation? The car explosion was bad enough, and they'd been fortunate no one got hurt.

She slipped out her chair, glanced out the window and spotted something that made her skin crawl. It looked like one of those toy drones she'd seen in stores across the country. It resembled a tiny spaceship, but this one had four things stuck to the bottom, and three of them had red tips.

Her heart pounding against her chest, she backed away from the window and quickly moved to the side. Seconds later the window shattered. Liv screamed and grabbed Patsy, throwing herself over the older woman as they both fell to the floor while small pieces of glass showered over them like rain. She found herself hyperventilating. This couldn't be happening. Things like this only happened in movies, not in real life.

What scared her the most was that the drone outside had three more of those things attached to the bottom. Taking a deep breath, Liv struggled to gain control of the situation. She would not allow Mr. Kale and those goons of his to hurt anyone at Mac's ranch. Lifting herself off Patsy, she stayed on her knees and took stock of their situation.

Patsy seemed to be in shock, but she didn't appear to be hurt outside of all the glass covering her body. Liv peered across the room and was stunned to see Cal had both dogs wrapped in his beefy arms, ready to protect them with his life, if his determined expression was anything to go by.

Okay, everyone in sight was all right. She took another deep breath. They had to get out of this room in case the drone fired off another shot. Just as she was helping Patsy to her feet, being careful of the glass, Mac and Rex burst into the kitchen. Relief hit her in a wave. Mac and his brother appeared okay.

Ducking with surprising agility and swift speed for a man of his size, Mac avoided the shattered window and took Patsy's other arm as they lifted her off the floor. Their eyes met, and his were filled with concern and worry. Guilt weighed heavily on her shoulders as they helped Patsy across the room, past the shattered window as quickly as possible and into the foyer.

Rex and Cal—with his arms full of dogs—followed close behind. Mac herded their small group to the center of the hallway in the middle of the house.

"I'm going outside to check on the ranch hands and to assess damage."

Liv grabbed the front of his shirt as fear rocketed

through her. "No! You can't do that." Her voice sounded shaky even to her own ears. "Th-there's a drone thing out there, and it might be waiting for someone to come outside. It h-has rockets attached to the bottom. Three of them have red tips."

Mac stared at her long and hard, and the guilt for the danger she'd brought to his doorstep was as invasive as a lethal disease. She had to get out of here, she thought desperately. She had to leave immediately. She couldn't go home to her ranch, either, placing her family in danger. She couldn't stay and put these fine people at risk.

Only Mr. Kale had the connections and power to send a drone after her. A drone could get to her anywhere, anytime. The magnitude of her situation hit her square in the chest. She had to go somewhere and hide. Somewhere no one could find her until she found proof against Mr. Kale and his goons.

Mac gently removed her tight grip from his shirt, and his eyes softened. "Liv, tell me what's going on. I can help you."

She lifted her chin and stared into soft brown eyes rimmed in gold, and she wanted to believe him so much it actually created an ache deep inside her. "No one can help me," she whispered.

In the middle of the most traumatic event of her life, her phone chirped, indicating she had a new text. Her stomach clenched in fear and her gut screamed that this text was connected to the drone attack. She pulled her hands out of the comforting warmth of Mac's and tugged her phone out of her pants pocket.

Her fingers shook so much, she barely got the text open. When she finally managed to accomplish that feat, she trembled not only at the message, but the fact that it completely disappeared within seconds, as if it had never been there. The phone slipped out of her frozen fingers and bounced off the hardwood floor. How could a text just disappear?

Mac bent over, picked up the phone and stared at the screen. His thick brows furrowed, and questioning eyes zeroed in on her.

"Rex, see to Patsy, then go outside and check on the boys," he said in a soothing Texas drawl, then added, "Cal, take care of the dogs. I need to talk to Liv."

Liv was aware of everyone responding to the quiet authority in his voice, but she stood still, as if she was frozen in time. Vaguely aware that she was now alone with Mac in the hallway, she jerked when callused fingers tenderly lifted her chin.

"Liv, please, talk to me."

Maybe it was the kindness in his voice, or the warmth of his fingers permeating the frozen tundra of her mind, but she finally came to life and her brain started sifting and sorting through everything that had transpired.

There was no doubt Mr. Kale knew where she was and his men were coming after her. With loaded guns. Literally. But was there anywhere she could go where they wouldn't find her? She didn't know whom to trust, and if she went to someone in authority, the people after her would make sure she landed in jail and became a sitting duck with no way to prove her innocence. She was an attorney and knew how the system worked.

There were good cops and there were bad ones. They'd make sure she was taken in by someone on their payroll.

"Liv," Mac said once again, "what was that on the phone? Did you receive a text message or email?"

Liv blinked and looked at Mac. Really looked at him. He was both kind and generous, even taking in people like Cal to help them get on their feet. He'd also kept her from being kidnapped. There weren't many people left in the world who reached out like Mac did to help people in need. Including herself.

Should she involve him in this? It wasn't his battle, but she was at her wit's end about what to do. He appeared strong enough to weather any storm, but she still hesitated. His whole family wasn't at the ranch, but she'd still be responsible for anything that happened to anyone here.

Before she made her decision, she decided to test his trust level. "I received a text message—" She hesitated but forged on, "But it disappeared immediately after I read it."

She watched him closely for any hint of disbelief and sighed inwardly when his expression hardened. Her stomach hit the top of her boots. He didn't believe her.

"Never mind. I have to gather my things and get out of here." She turned away from him, but he laid a gentle hand on her arm, which stopped her quicker than any show of force could ever have done.

"Liv, what did it say?"

His soft question crumbled her defenses. She had nowhere to go, and it felt like Mac was the only one standing between her and certain death. Turning around slowly, she took a deep breath.

"The text was from my boss. He said the first shot

was a warning and ordered me to come back to New York, or he said he'd destroy your ranch."

Mac tamped down the fury building in him at Liv's quiet reply. He wanted more than anything to believe her, but in order to prove her innocence—or guilt—he had to convince her to stay. Until he knew for sure either way, he would protect her.

Choosing his words carefully, he said, "Tell me why your boss wants you to come in and why he's threatening to destroy this ranch." Tear-filled honey-brown eyes gazed into his, and his protective instincts flared to life. He tamped down the emotions. He had to handle this with finesse.

Her lips trembled before she spoke. "I've worked so hard to get where I am. And now they're threatening to destroy everything."

It was probably a mistake, but Mac couldn't stop himself from pulling her into his arms. He rested his chin on the top of her head, and her body shuddered in his embrace before she finally quieted. With a sniffle, she pulled away and gave him a crooked smile.

"Thanks for the hug, but I'm okay now."

Embarrassment flickered across her face, and Mac surmised that in her profession she rarely revealed any type of vulnerability, but back to the business at hand. "Who's threatening to destroy everything, Liv?"

"I don't want any of your family or anyone working here hurt because of me."

"Well, now, you let me handle that," he said, his natural Texas twang showing itself. "I can protect what's mine."

He was relieved when she smiled, but it was short-lived. In the blink of an eye, she started pacing back and forth in the hallway, and Mac could almost see the wheels of her mind gaining traction. He envisioned her in a courtroom doing just that while facing a jury and hammering the final nail into the coffin of her opponent. She suddenly stopped in front of him.

She lifted a determined chin, and he was glad to see her fighting mantle back on. "Okay, here goes. The day before you found me on the side of the road with those goons—who, by the way, are privately employed my boss, Mr. Kale—I was in my cubicle working late at the office."

Mac grinned inwardly when she started pacing again, her clipped words exploding quickly and efficiently. The petite woman was a bundle of energy. Every aspect of her life was probably enhanced by that vitality.

She whipped around and glared at him as if daring him to believe her next words. "I heard Mr. Kale's voice coming from the corridor outside the room where I work, and I thought about letting him know I was there but figured he would never have a private conversation out in the open, outside his office." She paused, swallowed and whispered, "I heard Mr. Kale ask someone if they had covered all their tracks. The man responded in the affirmative, after which Mr. Kale said that now that they'd removed Burton from the equation, Mr. Stevenson would be free and clear. Mac, I was chosen to assist on that case, and Mr. Burton was the star witness. He was killed in a supposed hit-and-run the day before."

Mac digested the information. "It must have been an important case if your boss was willing to take the risk of removing a witness." Liv shuddered, and Mac stopped himself from comforting her. He had to have the truth.

"The last time I was at the ranch, Tempe sensed something was bothering me, and she was right. Lately, I've been noticing unusual things at work. Cases when the witnesses changed their stories once they were on the stand, employees of the firm retiring early with substantial retirement packages that seemed unusually high considering their positions."

She gazed at him, and the worry in her eyes almost unmanned him.

"Mac, I think the firm I work for isn't completely on the up-and-up."

"What about Mr. Burton? Why go to the extreme of getting rid of him?"

"Mr. Stevenson is a longtime client. He's an American international businessman who was accused, in layman's terms, of cheating his Turkish partner. They both invested heavily in a Turkish copper mine, and his Turkish partner claimed Mr. Stevenson was skimming money off the company. Mr. Stevenson's partner, Murat Akin, brought a suit against him."

Mac was baffled. "If it's just a case of skimming money, why the drastic measures of killing a witness?"

Liv lifted troubled eyes to his. "Mr. Burton, the star witness, worked for Mr. Stevenson in accounting. He was testifying against his own boss, and the evidence was solid. Mr. Stevenson was furious that one of his employees dared to turn against him and Mr. Stevenson would likely have gone to jail. Added to that, Mr. Kale would have lost a wealthy client."

Mac got to the heart of the matter. "Why is Mr. Kale trying to get rid of you?"

Liv took a deep breath. "They didn't know I was in the office working late. The building was pretty much empty by that time, it being Friday night. The lights were on, but that wasn't unusual. People were always forgetting to turn them off before they left. I heard Mr. Kale tell someone with them to turn off the lights to my office, and I hid until they moved down the hall. I gathered my things as quickly as possible, but I wasn't fast enough."

Mac's hands involuntarily fisted at the thought of Liv in that dangerous situation.

"The lights flashed on, almost blinding me, and one of the guys who tried to kidnap me on the side of the road tackled me in the walkway between the cubicles." Liv's lips curled at the corners, like she had a secret, and Mac stood there, amazed at her courage in the face of such a dire situation.

"After he jerked me to my feet, I started talking fast—something I'm very good at—and told the guy he didn't have to manhandle me, that I would go with him to speak with Mr. Kale, which is where he said he was taking me. I told him I had to make myself presentable and brush my hair. Instead, I grabbed a travel can of hair spray out of my purse and shot him right between the eyes."

Mac mentally applauded her ingenuity and courage in such a serious life and death situation.

"I got away and headed straight to my apartment to pack and pick up Misty. When we were safely in a taxi, I was checking my work emails to make sure I'd met a deadline for one of my pro bono cases, and I stumbled on an email I didn't write in my Sent box." She took a deep breath. "It looked like I hired a person to get rid of Mr. Burton. I couldn't call the police because of that incriminating email. When Mr. Kale's henchmen told him what had happened and they realized I'd overheard their conversation, he must have paid a hacker to put that email in my Sent box, because I certainly didn't send it," she added in a huff.

Her fury appeared real, and he wanted to believe her. Based on his dealings with Spider, he knew it was possible for someone to plant emails and make it appear as if they were sent by someone else. It was an intriguing story, but was it the truth? He needed more information. Much more.

"What, exactly, did the email say?"

"It said that I wanted Mr. Burton taken out and it should be made to look like an accident, and the payment would be sent in the usual manner after the deed was done."

Mac filed away the information. He'd take it apart later and examine not only the data but the accompanying emotions she revealed with every piece, because they were getting to the heart of the matter that was revealed in the FBI dossier.

"What happened then?" he asked, careful to conceal any emotion.

"I boarded my plane and rented a car at the airport when I arrived in Texas. The only safe place I could think to hide was the ranch. I knew the address could be easily linked to me, since I'm part owner, but I hoped the wide-open space would allow me a measure of safety. But Mr. Kale's goons caught up with my rental car before I could get there."

She gestured with both hands. "You know the rest of the story, because you caught them trying to kidnap me." A sheepish expression crossed her face. "I couldn't allow you to call the police because of those inflammatory emails. I need time to prove my innocence and gather evidence against Mr. Kale and any associates who may be involved in this." She took a deep breath. "Mac, I'm sorry I persuaded you to let me stay at your ranch. You see now why it's better that I leave. After what just happened, it's clear these men mean business."

Mac's brain was whirling faster than a roller coaster, but he rocked back on his heels and furrowed his brow. "Seems to me you need a safe place to stay and we need to find out what your boss is up to." And wasn't that the understatement of the year? The whirlwind in front of him took a long stride down the hall, then back again and stopped in front of him, splaying her arms wide.

"Don't you understand? You, your family or any of your employees could get hurt." She closed her eyes before opening them again, and her countenance softened. "I know you mean well, but I'm not sure you understand the magnitude of the situation. Mr. Kale is an international attorney, and his arms are far-reaching. Point of fact is him sending an armed drone here. Those things can go anywhere, anytime."

Mac stiffened at the implication that he couldn't protect her. She would be surprised if she knew he had connections with a lot of the big players, both on the national and international scenes, which was why he only contracted with the FBI instead of signing on permanently. He immensely disliked playing politics.

He'd been underestimated many times due to his upbringing and laid-back personality, and each time it had been to his advantage. This time would be no different, but he had to convince Liv to stay. He had to find out the truth, and she'd be dead inside a day if left to her own devices.

"As I told you before, let me worry about me and mine. I'll help you find out everything there is to know about your boss." She peered up at him boldly. Maybe adding a layer of information would be a deciding factor for her. "You remember Dean?"

The question seemed to catch her off guard, causing her brown-blond brows to snap together. "What? Who?"

"My brother. The youngest." When she didn't respond, he explained further. "I'm the oldest, then there's Zane, and after that came Fort, then Rex and finally Dean. We're all two years apart."

"Okay," she said slowly, and Mac knew he was losing her, so he started talking faster. "Well, Dean's a Navy SEAL, and I'll see if I can contact him. Maybe we can find out about those armed drones. He might be able to track down how a civilian was able to get their hands on them, or know someone who can."

He wouldn't really need Dean to find that information because he could do it himself, but he sure couldn't tell her he had contracted with the FBI, and the truth was, he would actually give Dean a call.

She scrunched up a nose that fit perfectly with her flawless face before squaring her shoulders and staring him in the eye. Mac grinned inside. He had her.

"My family has a lot of contacts, too. I'm going to call Tempe and let her know what's going on so they can be on guard, but I'd rather keep them out of this as much as possible, so I appreciate you calling Dean." She blew out a breath. "If you're sure you can keep everyone here safe, it'll give me time to do some research and investigate and hopefully find enough evidence against Mr. Kale to clear my name."

Relief that Liv would stay on the ranch and under his protection until this was resolved hit him square in the chest, so much so that he rubbed his hand above his stomach. Frowning at the absurd emotion, he dropped his arm and nodded. "If you'll let me, I'll help you with that chore."

Her gaze bored into him for a moment, then she slowly nodded. "I'd appreciate that, but the second anything even comes close to hurting someone on this ranch, I'm out of here."

Her cell phone buzzed, and her startled gaze shot to Mac. Pulling it out of her pocket slowly, she took the call. "Yes?"

Swallowing hard, she said, "It's Mr. Kale. He wants to know if you're with me and asked me to put the speaker on."

He nodded for her to do as instructed, and a smooth, cultivated voice filtered through the tiny speaker. "Mr. Dolan, I'm sure by now you understand the magnitude of the situation Miss Calloway has gotten herself into. We have proof that she's responsible for the death of a witness in a case our firm is handling. It would be to your benefit to turn her over to us. We're one of the best law firms in the country, and we'll do our utmost to defend her against any charges the police may file against her."

Liv's face lost all color, but instead of turning pleading eyes in his direction, as Mac expected after Mr. Kale's accusations, Liv straightened her shoulders and looked Mac in the eye, awaiting his decision with a dignity that made his respect for her soar. At the moment, Mac didn't know who was telling the truth, but he did know one thing—Kale had tried to kidnap and kill Liv, and there was no way he would turn her over to anyone until he had proof one way or the other.

"Tell me one thing," Mac drawled into the phone.

"Yes?" replied a more clipped voice this time.

"Where would a fine, upstanding lawyer like yourself manage to put his hands on a drone that's illegal to the public?"

Silence, then, "It's a pity that we can't come to an understanding. Miss Calloway is guilty of murder, and you can thank her for anything that may happen on your ranch or to your family. From what you've said, someone wants her out of the way and will stop at nothing to achieve that goal."

The phone disconnected, and Liv lifted her chin. "He's the one doing all this, but he's smart enough to keep from incriminating himself."

Before Mac had a chance to respond, their startled gazes met when Rex frantically yelled Mac's name from somewhere downstairs.

SEVEN

Liv stayed right on Mac's heels as they followed Barnie's earsplitting howls to a room at the back of the house she hadn't yet had a chance to explore. She bumped into his back when he came to a dead stop at the entrance to what looked like a TV room.

"Sorry," she apologized to Mac half-heartedly as she scanned the room.

A massive television was mounted on the wall, and there were four rows of actual theater seats placed strategically in front of the screen. Patsy and Rex stood staring out a window, and Cal sat in one of the oversize seats with both dogs bound in his thick arms.

Cal released Barnie, and the coonhound raced to the window, baying frantically and pawing the windowsill. Liv's stomach roiled as she followed Mac to the window, remembering Mr. Kale's implied threat that she would be responsible for anything that happened on Mac's ranch.

Feeling Mac stiffen beside her, she slowly stared out the window and recoiled when she spotted the beautiful white airplane she'd noticed upon arrival being devoured in flames. She placed a hand on her stomach when her body threatened to eject her last meal.

"Mac, whose plane is that?" she whispered around the large lump threatening to choke off her airway.

It startled her when he whipped around, and the hard flash in his eyes caused her to take a cautious step back. This wasn't the laid-back cowboy she'd come to know. The man standing in front of her was a warrior in full battle mode.

"The plane is mine, and your boss just made this personal." His words came out sharp and clipped, and Liv took another step back.

In a slight daze, she jerked when two strong hands lightly gripped both her arms.

"Liv, do you understand? I'm not only going to help you clear your name, but I'm going to bury your boss. He targeted my house, the people in my care and now my plane. He's touched me and mine, and he'll pay for that."

Liv slowly raised her head and stared deeply into those darkened brown eyes, searching for the truth. Could she trust him? Did he really believe her story? She didn't know, but there was nowhere to run and she'd have to take a chance.

He wrapped her in strong arms and whispered in her ear, a smile in his voice. "Don't you worry about that plane, darlin'. I've got another one hidden in a hangar here on the ranch. It's small, but it gets the job done."

Another plane? The information snapped her out of her tumultuous thoughts, and she pulled out of his embrace, leaving the warmth he'd provided—warmth she mourned the loss of as soon as the cool air flowed between them.

Straightening to her full five feet five inches—she would have given anything for her heels to make her taller—she addressed him, but trod carefully. "Mac, I apologize for the damage to your house and plane—"

He waved a hand in the air, interrupting her. "I have insurance, and the plane isn't near any other structure sitting out there by itself on the runway."

She cleared her throat. "Before we go any further, there's already been a lot of damage to your parents' house, not to mention the danger to its occupants. This is becoming both dangerous and expensive for you."

Before Mac had a chance to respond, Liv's attention was diverted when Rex stifled a half laugh, half snort. Mac's younger brother appeared to be having a hard time containing his mirth. Maybe she could get a real reaction from Rex.

"Is there something you would like to add, Rex?" she asked in her crisp attorney voice.

He lost control and laughed out loud. "Not really, it's just that I think my brother has finally met his match."

Mac shot him a look that Liv couldn't decipher before directing those warm eyes back to her. "Don't mind my brother, Liv, and don't worry about the expense. I'm a financial planner, and I make plenty of money. Between that and the insurance, there's no need to worry."

Rex snorted again, but Liv ignored the prison preacher and made up her mind. She had nowhere to go, and she had to find evidence against Mr. Kale. The sooner that happened, the better. Mac had said he could protect what was his, so she'd leave him to it. When she cleared her name, she and Misty could go back to New York and she could get her career back on track. She would douse the tiny flame deep inside her that flickered to life every time she interacted with Mac, because she wasn't ready for a relationship. She wanted to work for the Department of Justice, and she didn't have time for a family until she met her career goals.

She pasted on a smile and walked toward Cal, plucking Misty out of his arms. "Well, that's nice." She peered around the room, feeling out of sorts. Patsy's eyes were narrowed when Liv glanced at her, and Liv dearly hoped she hadn't lost the instant connection she'd felt with the older woman when they met. Rex's eyes were still filled with mirth.

Liv nodded stiffly at Cal. "Thank you for taking care of Misty." She looked at the room at large. "I need to do some research." What she needed was to find some evidence against Mr. Kale. Her gaze met Mac's. "Unless there's something I can do to help with the mess in the kitchen or," she added weakly, "the fire outside."

Mac slowly shook his head, but his eyes never left hers. "The boys'll take care of everything. I'll see you to your room," he said before gently taking her by the elbow and leading her away from prying ears.

So many things had happened so fast, she needed time to think through all the unexpected events and sort her thoughts, but Mac's soft touch scattered her brain cells to the wind. He didn't speak until they'd climbed the stairs and stopped in front of her room.

"Liv, I meant what I said. Your boss has now made this personal, and you have me and any resources I have available at your disposal."

Liv peered into warm brown eyes that begged her to trust him, and she wanted to with every fiber of her being. Unfortunately, she inherently knew, deep down inside where she hid her most secret dreams, that this man could be her downfall. She needed time to regroup.

He leaned so close she smelled peppermint on his breath, and she automatically lifted Misty higher in her arms, creating a perfect barrier.

He gave her a crooked smile and stepped back. "I'll see to the damage outside and in the kitchen, then call Dean and see if he has any idea how to find out who might've had an opportunity to get their hands on an armed drone. He always has his ear to the ground. We can compare notes on what we learn after supper."

He ambled away, and Liv straightened her shoulders, opened her bedroom door, set Misty on the floor and grabbed her laptop before heading to Mac's mother's office. She had to find evidence against Mr. Kale, and she wanted to do it before someone at Mac's ranch got hurt—or worse.

With Barnie at his side, Mac stared at his Cessna Citation—a beautiful nine-passenger plane he'd just gotten back from repairs—as it burned to the ground. His lips twisted wryly. Liv's sister, Tempe, was the cause of the repairs, due to a little incident she and her new husband had had while flying to Florida last summer after she borrowed his plane. The Calloway sisters seemed to wreak havoc on his property, but that wasn't important. He had enough money to handle everything.

What was important was the gall of her boss, thinking he could come after Liv on Mac's turf and get away with it. Rex came up alongside him, and the two men stared at the flames devouring the plane.

Mac's thoughts must have been written on his face, because Rex intoned dryly, "I haven't seen you this interested in anything in two years."

It had been two years since his divorce, and Mac wanted to smack his smug little brother. "Leave it alone, Rex. I'll find out the truth about Miss Calloway, and she'll either go back to New York and resume her career or she'll be in the slammer. Either way, what you're thinking isn't gonna happen."

Rex released a put-upon sigh. His preacher brother could make his thoughts known without ever saying a word, which was why he was so good at his vocation. People tended not to want to disappoint him.

"That guilt-induced sigh won't work on me. I grew up with you and know every trick in your book."

They stood in silence for a moment, but his nosy brother never stayed quiet for long. "Liv sure did grow into a nice-looking woman." Mac agreed, but didn't comment. "Seems smart, too."

Mac whirled on his brother, his fists clinched. "Give it up, Rex. It's not gonna happen."

Rex held both hands up in surrender. "You can't blame a brother for trying. I just want you to be happy."

"I am happy," Mac growled. But was he? He made plenty of money, took the occasional mission from the FBI and handled search and rescue missions with Barnie. It was enough, he convinced himself. It would have to be.

"Why don't you worry about your own love life and leave me in peace, and don't you have a job to get back to?"

Rex's white teeth gleamed in a wide, knowing smile as he walked backward. "Right." He turned toward the driveway where his truck was parked, but threw one last shot over his shoulder. "Let me know if you need any help. The ladies love me."

Mac went so far as to bend over and grab some dirt off the runway, but he restrained himself from throwing it at his retreating brother, who was laughing out loud. He opened his hand, released the dirt and turned back to the plane. Several of the ranch hands were trying to put out the fire, but Mac told them to let it burn. The fire couldn't spread anywhere, and he wasn't willing to risk anyone getting injured.

He'd have to call the law and have them file a report for insurance purposes, but he highly suspected the armed drone had done the damage. His security system hadn't reported any breaches other than the drone. He needed information on how much firepower could be packed into one of those things. Maybe he did need to call Dean. His youngest brother was a Navy SEAL, but Mac often wondered if Dean was involved in more within the SEALs than he let on. They had plenty of secret ops.

Ten minutes later, back in his computer room, he did an online search, but he still had questions. Hoping Dean was somewhere he could receive calls, he punched in his number, heard several clicks that he assumed was the line diverting the call around the world so it couldn't be traced, then heard a familiar voice that filled him with warmth and a flood of good memories.

"This better be important, bro, 'cause I'm a tad busy here," Dean whispered into the phone.

Mac got straight to the point, as brothers tended to do. “Can a small drone carry enough firepower to blow up a Cessna?”

Silence filled the airways. “What have you gotten yourself into, big brother? Does it have anything to do with Olivia Calloway?”

Mac’s nostrils flared. His family knew he contracted out with the FBI periodically, but Dean shouldn’t know any particulars. Hopefully Dean would be home soon and they could have a nice brother-to-brother chat, which usually included some roughhousing. “And how do you know about that?”

“Let’s just say I tend to keep up with things that concern the family. Talk.”

Mac heard gunfire popping from what sounded like a fairly safe distance away and figured Dean was in the middle of something he couldn’t talk about, so he got straight to the point. “Since you seem to know everything anyway, Liv is staying here at the ranch for the time being, and I’m pretty sure her boss sent an armed drone in and just blew up my Cessna. The big one,” he added for good measure.

Dean spoke low and fast. “Sounds like he got hold of a UCAV combat drone. It can carry up to four small-diameter bombs. The unmanned combat aerial vehicles aren’t available to civilians unless her boss has contacts in high places. It could have been diverted through another country. Stuff like that happens every day.”

Mac heard the weariness in his brother’s voice, but he trod lightly. “Dean, are you able to come home for a visit soon?”

His words tight, Dean said, “Not yet. I have something I need to take care of first. I'll apply for some time after that."

Mac knew not to push. There was something, probably something dangerous, going on with his brother, but all Mac could do was to pray for his continued safety. "Thanks for the info. It'd be great if you could make it home for Easter."

"Maybe," Dean said, and the line went dead.

Mac said a quick prayer for his brother's safety and turned to his computer. He pulled up his email and typed a long message to the person known only as Spider, asking them to look into the email sitting in Liv's Sent box that she claimed had been put there by someone else. He offered Spider a bonus above what he usually paid them if they could track where the email actually originated from. That would go a long way in proving Liv's innocence, and he found himself hoping that she was, indeed, innocent. He clicked the send button and leaned back in his swivel chair, staring at the screen, even though he knew it might be an hour or days before he heard back from his contact if Spider was working on something else.

Lost deep in thought, he jerked out of his chair when he heard Liv frantically calling her dog. "Misty!"

EIGHT

Liv ran down the stairs and called her dog's name. Misty usually stayed right next to her as she worked, and it wasn't like the dog to slip away. She briefly poked her head into every room, and her heart pounded in fear when she noticed the front door wasn't closed. It stood open just wide enough for a small dog to slip through. Throwing it all the way open, she screamed Misty's name. At her side, Barnie released an ear-splitting bay at the same time.

Misty only weighed eight pounds. If she went outside, a horse or steer could easily kill her. Liv started trembling when she thought of all the things on a ranch that could hurt her baby.

The heavy tread of boots caught her attention, and Mac approached at the same time Patsy stuck her head out of the kitchen.

"What is it? What's happened?" Mac demanded, deep concern etched into his face.

Mac might think she was overreacting, but Liv didn't care. "It's Misty. I left your mother's office door open and after briefly checking the downstairs, I realized the front door wasn't completely closed. I..." Liv struggled to hold the tears at bay. "I'm afraid she went outside. She's a city dog. She doesn't know to stay away from horses and cattle. She could walk right under one and they could step on her and—"

Mac's strong hands on her shoulders stopped her midsentence. "Liv, calm down. We'll find your dog. But we have to be careful. Misty could have been lured outside in order to get you to come out after her."

"But she could be anywhere," she babbled on.

Mac glanced at Patsy. "Patsy, check the house from top to bottom, and I'll look outside." Mac glanced back at Liv. "They'll more likely target you than me."

Patsy gave Mac a sharp nod and sent a sympathetic glance to Liv. At least it appeared as if she hadn't lost Patsy's friendship. Mac dropped his hands from her shoulders and stepped outside. Liv regained her equilibrium and ran after him.

He stopped short. "Stay in the house. It's unlikely due to battery life, but the drone may still be out here. I'll shoot it down if it comes after me."

The hard point of Mac's eyes softened, and Liv realized he was willing to risk his life to save her dog. An arrow pinged the middle her heart, but she quickly subdued it. She'd think about his willingness to sacrifice later. At the moment, her Texas grit reasserted itself.

"Not without me, you're not."

He opened his mouth, then snapped it shut. Her determination must have shown in her face. "Stay close to me," he ordered, then looked at his dog, whose ears were flapping back and forth between them as they talked. "Barnie, with me," he commanded. Mac grabbed something out of the foyer closet and took off out the front door and down the steps.

Liv searched the sky as they stepped outside, half expecting to see the drone aimed straight at them, but there were only puffy clouds enhanced by a beautiful light blue sky. As they entered the barn to check whether the ranch hands had spotted Misty, a loud, mournful bay filled the air.

Her heart in her throat, Liv ran outside ahead of Mac, only to stop short when she spotted Barnie at the far side of the paddock, his head lifted in another loud bay. A scrap of material lay on the ground, and Liv didn't even realize she was running until she reached Mac's dog. Afraid to look, she slowly lowered her gaze and bent over like an old woman, retrieving a piece of the Western outfit Misty had been wearing.

She stood there staring at it, feeling strangely emotionally detached as she wondered if her dog was still alive. Vaguely aware that Mac had come up beside her, she whispered her worst nightmare. "Are there still coyotes in Texas? Or do you think Mr. Kale's goons have my baby?"

When Mac didn't answer, she noted rapid movement off to her side. Mac was strapping something onto Barnie's back. It was a black and red vest with the words *Search and Rescue* printed boldly on both sides.

Mac snapped the vest closed, and Barnie turned into a different dog right before her eyes. His stature was perfectly erect, and he focused entirely on Mac. Mac's gaze found hers, and pure resolve filled his expression.

"Barnie's a fully trained rescue dog. We'll find

Misty. Alive." The last word sounded like an edict and pulled Liv out of her immobility.

"What can I do?"

Mac's lips lifted at the corners in a ghost of a smile. "Since I know you won't stay here, you'll have to keep up."

Misty was alive. She'd hold on to that until proven otherwise. "Go! I'm right behind you." She watched in fascination as Mac held the piece of clothing from Misty's outfit under Barnie's nose.

"Barnie. Find!"

Liv stayed quiet as Barnie immediately went to work, his nose to the ground. He followed a scent only he could smell all around the paddock, then he took off across the plain, big ears flapping. Mac started running, and Liv took off after him.

Fighting prickly scrub brush, she ran as fast as she could. She didn't know how long they'd been running when Barnie came to a dead stop halfway between Mac's family's ranch and the foothills guarding the Chisos Mountains. The dog circled in the same spot for a minute and then lifted his head and bayed loudly.

Afraid to the core of her being, Liv could only watch as Mac bent over and praised Barnie. It took a few minutes for him to settle the dog down. His mouth in a grim line, he gazed at Liv.

"The scent trail stops here."

Her heart hammered against her chest, and she wanted to scream, but instead she took a deep breath. "It can't end here," she said out loud, somehow hoping that would make the statement true.

Mac stepped toward her, sorrow filling his eyes. "I'm

sorry, Liv. I've never seen Barnie get so upset over losing a scent." His lips curled sadly. "I think he designated himself as Misty's protector."

Liv turned in a tight circle and gestured wildly with her hands. "She couldn't have just disappeared off the face of the earth."

Just as Mac opened his mouth, no doubt to offer sympathy, Barnie let out a piercing bay and tore off toward a foothill. A stunned expression covered Mac's face, but Liv took off after her only hope of finding her baby. The cool air slapped her in the face, and she stumbled a couple of times, but she refused to give up. Misty had to be okay. The dog had been with her through good times and bad. Liv had shed more than one tear into her soft fur. She was the only one Liv ever allowed herself to reveal her vulnerabilities to.

Mac came hard on her heels and overtook her. Boots were great for a ranch, but they definitely weren't made for running. She saw Mac and Barnie approach the closest foothill and then heard the sweetest sound and one that calmed her racing heart—Misty barking her head off. Barnie must have heard the dog's terrified cries from a distance.

When Liv caught up with them, she slowed down and took in the scene. Misty was perched on a ledge halfway up the steep hill. It wasn't near as steep as the huge mountains in the background, but it was still dangerous. Shielding her eyes, she peered up, relief hitting her in waves. It didn't look as if Misty was injured, but the small dog sounded terrified. Liv wanted Misty in her arms as soon as possible.

Mac turned with a huge smile on his face. "She's

okay," he said, then looked toward the sky. "But let's hurry. Kale's men may have lured her outside and then placed her here. We could be sitting ducks."

At Liv's startled intake of breath, Mac followed her line of vision and watched his dog. He was shocked a second time at Barnie's unusual behavior. His normally calm coonhound was climbing the foothill, one sure-footed step at a time. Keeping his pistol at the ready, Mac watched as his trusty companion risked his own life to save Liv's dog.

Misty's eyes stayed glued on Barnie as Mac's dog slowly made his way to the ledge. Mac held his breath when Barnie climbed above ledge, leaned over and solidly clamped his teeth on the back of Misty's outfit. He easily lifted the papillon off the ledge and gingerly made his way back down the hill.

Mac grinned when Miss New Yorker ran over to them, dropped to her knees in the dirt, wrapped both dogs in her arms and rained kisses all over Barnie's face.

"You sweet dog. You're a hero, you hear me? I'm going to buy you a steak when we get back to the house. You deserve that and more, and I'm going to have Babette create you a special outfit. Maybe it'll even have a cape on the back."

Mac's grin widened as he watched his highly trained coonhound bask in Liv's adoration. His dog finally deigned to mosey over to Mac, a doggie smile on his face. Mac leaned over and praised him. "Good job, buddy. Let's go home and get you a treat."

Barnie's ears immediately perked up. Liv stood off

to the side, Misty wrapped tightly in her arms. The dog was still trembling after the harrowing experience, but Liv had a big smile on her face.

"Thank you for finding Misty," she said, tears welling up in her eyes.

Mac suspected that Liv rarely allowed anyone to see her vulnerability, and it touched him in a place that had long been dormant. A place he hadn't ever expected to revive. He couldn't allow that to happen, at least not with the woman standing in front of him—a woman who would firmly place her career before marriage and babies.

"You're welcome," he said and scanned the horizon. "We better get back. I don't think that drone had enough battery life to still be hanging around, but there may be men stationed out here, waiting for us." He immediately regretted wiping the smile off her face, but maybe it was better this way.

"Of course, you're right," she said and started back the way they came.

After Barnie's vest was removed to let the dog know he was off duty, his coonhound stayed close to both the woman and dog. Mac blew out a breath. He didn't blame his dog, he thought as he fell in behind them. He wouldn't mind staying close to Liv if circumstances were different.

Now was as good a time as any to dig deeper into Liv's life. Not for personal reasons, he reminded himself, but to discover if she was innocent or guilty of murder. She certainly didn't strike him as a killer, but as he'd discovered in the past, the drive for money and success could tempt a person to do things they wouldn't normally do.

He caught up with her and matched his long strides to her shorter ones. "I heard through the grapevine that Tempe and Ewen discovered oil on your property." She had loosened her hold on Misty but didn't appear ready to release her any time soon.

She snorted, and it sounded odd coming from such a petite and sophisticated woman. "You're right. We discovered shale oil, but it's going to be a while before we see any profit from the endeavor. Ewen is helping Tempe connect with the right people. Shale oil is harder to extract, and it's more complicated than regular oil."

Staying alert to their surroundings, Mac processed that bit of information. Liv wasn't receiving money now, but she would in the future. "So how long have you been working for the firm in New York?" he asked in a lazy drawl. He'd always found his laid-back manner caused people to relax and he got more information that way.

She shot him a glance that told him his attempt at a soft interrogation wasn't working. He suppressed a grin. She was a smart gal, and he liked sharp women.

"You want information because Mr. Kale has now made this personal to you?" she asked, repeating what he'd said back at the house.

"Yep. That about sums it up."

She took several steps before stopping and facing him. "I'll tell you everything if you'll answer one question for me."

He nodded slowly and smiled. The woman was fast on her feet. She'd keep him on his toes, and he loved a good challenge. "All right. If it's within reason."

"Why did you agree to let me and Misty stay at your house?"

He rocked back on his heels as her eyes narrowed. "Well, now, it seems to me that's a delicate question that calls for a delicate answer."

She raised a manicured brow. "Well, now," she said, mimicking him, "it seems to me that's an evasive answer. And you should never play poker. I'm an attorney trained to detect mannerisms and speech in order to ascertain whether someone is telling the truth."

Mac's toes hit the dirt, and he grinned. Yep, the lady was sharp, and she tickled him pink. "Maybe I met a beautiful lady I knew when she was a kid and I wanted to help her out and get to know her a little better."

Her eyes cut to his. "Have you ever been married, Mac?"

He stopped in his tracks and growled, "What does that have to do with anything?"

She smiled sweetly, but her eyes were those of a shark seeking supper. "You said you wanted us to get to know each other better, and I thought I'd reciprocate."

"There you go using big words," he answered evasively.

"I'll take that as a yes." She raised one brow. "I assume since you're living with your parents that you're divorced, and based on your reaction, that it wasn't amicable."

Maybe he didn't like smart women after all. "Yes, on both counts," he grumbled, but his answer did make her smile, a real one this time, and it felt like the sun had just come out after a long, dreary rain.

Misty licked Liv's chin, and she cooed to the tiny

dog. "Even though you won't give me a straight answer as to why you allowed me and Misty to stay with you, I'll still answer your question. I went to college at Harvard, then attended Harvard Law School. I graduated with honors and easily landed a job with Kale, Kale & Johnston. I've been with the firm for four years."

"So you're one smart cookie." It wasn't a question.

She actually blushed, but forged ahead. "My ten-year career plan was right on track until my run-in with Mr. Kale and his goons."

Mac briefly wondered if her ten-year goals included getting rid of clients so she could win a big case. Trying to sound as casual as possible, he asked, "And what are your career plans?"

She came to a stop and faced him, radiating excitement and determination. "Within six more years, my goal is to be working for the Department of Justice."

Well, now, wasn't that something, Mac thought. He happened to be personally acquainted with someone working in that department. "Is that so?"

"Yes," she said, but then her face crumpled. "Unless Mr. Kale ruins my chances." She took a deep breath. "Mac, I really don't care why you're allowing me and Misty to stay here, but I do appreciate your offer to help. I have to clear my name, or my career is finished."

The irony of the situation hit Mac full force. Even if he did have designs on Liv, which he didn't, if he helped her prove her innocence, he was in essence ensuring she'd have her heart's desire: a career over living on a ranch in the middle of nowhere and having a family. Not that it mattered, because she wouldn't ever be happy in his world.

He shook off the disturbing thought. Why was he even thinking along those lines? His job was to find out if she was guilty or innocent, and that would be the end of his involvement.

Barnie lifted his head and released a long, harrowing bay.

Mac looked to the sky, and what he saw had him automatically shoving Liv to the ground while pulling out his pistol in one swoop. The drone was back, and they were sitting targets.

NINE

Barnie's loud bay startled Liv, and the next thing she knew, she was being shoved roughly to the ground. She landed on her right shoulder but managed to hold on to Misty. Pain radiated down her arm, but she ignored it and tightened her grip on her small, precious bundle. She twisted her neck and glanced skyward to where Mac was pointing his gun, and her blood turned to ice.

The drone was back, and it still had two red-tipped missiles attached to the bottom. The first one at the house must not have been a bomb—more of an attempt to get her outside of the house and a better target. In her opinion, Mr. Kale would likely prefer to keep the possible collateral damage of other people getting killed to a minimum to make things easier on himself. But she had no doubt that the other three were completely armed bombs after she'd seen Mac's plane burn.

"Liv," Mac yelled, "stay put. I'm going to shoot it down."

Liv froze. Shoot it down? Would the missiles explode? She didn't have time to do anything but roll over face-first with Misty cuddled in her arms a second before she heard Mac's gun fire.

The sound of an explosion filled the air and tiny, hot embers penetrated the back of her shirt, but they barely burned. She was so scared, she couldn't move, but then a big tongue licked her jaw and broke the spell. She peered up into Barnie's sappy face.

Reaching up, she patted him. "You saved us again, Barnie." She heard the shakiness in her own voice and cleared her throat. Mac gently shoved Barnie to the side and knelt down beside her.

"Liv, are you okay?" Worry laced his words. "I'm sorry I had to push you down."

Spitting dirt out of her mouth, she rolled onto her back and stared at the beautiful, clear sky. "They really want to kill me, don't they? I'm sure they somehow lured Misty outside to make me an easier target." She'd already known this, but it was like the danger she was in had really hit home. She peered into Mac's concerned face.

He rocked back on his heels. "Yep, not much doubt about that."

After pushing herself to her feet while hanging on to Misty, she rubbed her shoulder.

"Are you hurt?"

"It's okay." She forced a weak smile. "Better my shoulder than something worse."

"Yeah, well, I think we'd better get back to the house if you can walk okay."

"I'm more than ready to get back to the house."

Barnie approached, lifted his head and sniffed all

around Misty. Liv smiled. "That's so sweet. Barnie wants to make sure Misty is okay."

Mac wore an odd expression as he stared at his dog.

"What?" Liv asked.

Mac shook his head. "I've never seen him act this way."

Liv gave Misty a smooch on the top of her head. "I think he loves Misty."

Liv wondered at the speculative look Mac sent her. "Why would he do that?" he asked, as if the conversation was about humans instead of the dogs. "It would never work. Misty's all city, and Barnie's an old coonhound."

If it was a hint at their differences, Liv didn't want to go there, so she changed the subject. "Did you ever talk to your brother Dean about the drone and how a civilian might have acquired one?" she asked as they started moving toward Mac's house. She appreciated that he shortened his long stride to keep pace with her.

"Sure did. Dean wasn't happy with the knowledge of a drone in the hands of a civilian. He said someone had to have a lot of clout in order to purchase one. Is there anything else you can add about the case you were working on and your client?"

Liv took a minute to pull her thoughts together and rubbed her shoulder again. Mac looked like he was going to say something, and she dropped her hand, hopefully avoiding another inquiry into her slight injury.

"Nothing I didn't tell you earlier. It's just—" she stopped walking and faced him "—we have to find a way to stop Mr. Kale, but he's a smart man to have achieved such a high level of success."

"What's your opinion of the client's innocence or guilt?" he asked mildly.

"That would have been for a jury to decide," she retorted sharply. Mac probably didn't realize it, but he'd hit a raw nerve that had been bothering her for a while now. She had to defend the clients assigned to her to the best of her ability, whether they were innocent or guilty.

A thoughtful expression crossed his face. "Can I ask you a question?"

"Within reason."

"What made you decide go into law? You're a smart woman. You could have done anything."

The house came into view, and she stopped suddenly, taking issue with his implication. "Practicing law is a noble profession. I know there's a lot of problems with the system, which is why I plan to work for the Department of Justice. I'd like a chance to help make the system better, and Mr. Kale will be held accountable if it's the last thing I ever do."

Her fighting spirit had returned, and it felt good, but she took a deep breath to calm down. It didn't matter what Mac thought of her profession, but she really wanted him to understand something she'd never tried to put into words.

"I grew up with a sense of right and wrong instilled deeply inside me. I got into law because I want to help people navigate a complicated system when they find themselves in an untenable situation."

He pushed back the brim of his cowboy hat, and

his brown eyes pierced her. "And is that what you're doing?"

His response hit that same sore spot she'd thought about earlier, and she stroked Misty's soft fur to calm herself down. Pasting on a bright smile, she said, "That's why I want to work for the Department of Justice. Being in that position will give me enough clout to help the small guys on a larger scale."

Dropping her gaze when he just kept staring at her, she started walking forward. She wanted to get away from Mac and those questioning eyes that made her doubt herself. She had a ten-year plan, and nothing or no one was going to sway her from the goal she'd set for herself when she entered college.

They walked in silence until they got close to the house. Liv stopped when she spotted a very fancy sports car—yes, that was a Lamborghini—sitting in the drive, and Mac's long strides took him past her as he headed straight for the vehicle. Curious, Liv followed him to the vehicle just as a long pair of legs clad in black leather pants swung out of the driver's side and a pair of what looked like lizard-skin boots hit the ground.

She stopped and her chin dropped when the guy ducked his head, stepped out of the car and stood grinning at Mac. Without stopping to think, she blurted, "You're *that* Fort? The famous baseball player?"

Despite wanting to herd her into the house because they were still out in the open, Mac couldn't stop himself from asking, "You keep up with baseball?"

Without taking her eyes off his way-too-smooth-talking younger sibling, she said, "Not at all, but—"

she spoke to Fort more than Mac "—I've seen all your jean ads on TV and social media. I just didn't connect you to the Dolan boys."

Mac studied Fort. His brother took after their dad, the same as Zane, Dean and Mac did. Rex was the only one who took after their mother. They were all well over six feet tall and had dark brown hair and brown eyes. Nothing special, but the one thing Fort did have in abundance was charisma. That's probably why he had so many endorsements. With all his extracurriculars, Mac sometimes wondered how Fort found time to actually play baseball. But he knew how much Fort made on all those commercials because his brother was one of his financial planning clients.

Before moving them toward the house, Mac asked, "What are you doing here? Baseball season is over, and I thought you were busy filming your commercials."

Fort observed Liv for a moment, then turned to Mac and grinned, revealing perfectly aligned, whitened teeth. In the slow, Texas drawl his fans went wild over, he said, "Just thought I'd stop by and visit my big brother, but I can leave if I'm interrupting something important."

Mac read the weariness behind the too-bright smile on Fort's face and sighed inwardly. His brothers always seemed to gravitate to the ranch and their big brother when they were having problems. Mac didn't mind for the most part, but this wasn't a good time. Someone was trying to kill Liv, and Rex had dropped Cal off at the ranch.

"Of course you're not leaving," Liv interjected with enthusiasm before Mac could respond. "Mac is just, uh, helping me out with a small problem." She stuck out her hand. "You may not remember me, but I'm Liv Calloway. I grew up on the Calloway ranch, not far from here."

Mac snorted, and Liv glared at him. He couldn't help himself as he responded incredulously, "A *small* problem?"

She totally ignored Mac and directed her conversation to Fort. "This is Misty."

"Why, she's darlin'," he said and scratched the dog's tiny head. "Thought about getting me a dog, but with being on the road so much of the year, it's not too practical."

Time to cut the introduction party short. "Liv, we need to get you inside where it's safe, and I need to see if Dean has come across anything," he said, sending her a meaningful glance.

She stiffened and nodded curtly. "You're right. Fort, I'll talk to you later if you plan to stay."

Mac felt like a heel when worry clouded her eyes and she walked away, Misty in her arms and Barnie on her heels, but he reacted automatically when she disappeared into the house and a big fist plowed into his right arm. His return uppercut was blocked, and Fort grinned as he held Mac's arm in a tight grip.

"You're getting slow in your old age, big brother."

Mac shook his head, and Fort released his arm. Rubbing the bruised area, he asked, "What was that for?"

Fort raised a dark brow. "That was for wiping the smile off Liv's face." He paused. "It's no wonder you can't find a woman if that's how you treat 'em."

Mac counted to ten before addressing his younger

brother. "I am not courting Liv. She has a problem I'm helping her out with. A dangerous problem."

Fort contemplated that for a moment. "I assume since she's staying here and not at the Calloway ranch that it has something to do with your contract work with the FBI."

Mac glared at him. "I only informed the family of my connection with the FBI so you would be aware in case something followed me home. You're not to mention it again. Especially in front of Liv."

Fort held up his hands in surrender. "You can trust me. My lips are sealed." He studied the toes of his very expensive lizard-skin boots, then lifted his head. "Well, then, if you're not courtin' Miss Calloway, you won't mind if I ask her out myself."

Mac rolled his eyes skyward. "Fort, this is not a competition, not like when we were in high school. This is real and Liv's life is on the line. Besides, I thought you mentioned a woman in the picture."

His brother's gaze shifted away, and Mac sighed inwardly yet again. He knew something was up when Fort dug the toe of that expensive boot into the Texas dirt. "You might as well tell me."

Lifting his head and staring at the horizon, Fort started talking. "Well, it's like this. You know Dan Madden, the team owner, well, he has a sister named Charlene. Dan is real protective of her, doesn't like the idea of her dating a ballplayer, but that's only part of the problem."

"So, what's the rest of the problem?" Mac asked, impatience coursing through him. He didn't mind helping his brothers, but surely they didn't expect him to fix their personal lives.

"The thing is, Charlene is kind of a bookworm, and she doesn't even like baseball."

Mac prodded him. "And?"

Fort lifted his chin, and a puzzled expression crossed his face. "She's not impressed by my skills on the field or the large amounts of money I make doing commercials."

Mac deliberated for a few minutes. "Seems to me you need to figure out what *will* impress the lady."

Exasperated, Fort threw his hands in the air. "Big lot of help you are."

Mac had had enough. "Yes, well, I have enough on my plate right now. You staying or leaving?" Mac asked shortly.

He didn't miss the glint in Fort's eye but chose to ignore it. "I believe I'll hang around for a few days."

Mac turned to go to the house. He couldn't get Liv's worried expression out of his mind. He had been too abrupt. "Fine. I've got work to do." Mac ignored Fort when his brother slammed his car door closed and followed Mac into the house. Anxious to check on Liv, Mac took the stairs two at a time, ignoring Patsy's warm greeting to Fort behind him.

Liv had been through a lot today. She'd handled the drone attack well—better than he would have ever expected—but if she was innocent, it was his job to keep her safe. He slowed as he approached the door of his mother's office. Liv was talking on the phone, and he didn't want to intrude on her privacy, but he started moving forward again. What if he could learn something useful? His allegiance was to the FBI, not to her.

Her voice rose in volume as he got closer, and there was no mistaking her words. “Tempe, I’m telling you now. Yes, I’ve told you everything, and I’m fine. I just wanted to warn you in case Mr. Kale decides to go after my family. No, you do not need to come over here.”

Mac stopped right outside the door and continued to listen to Liv’s end of the conversation with her sister.

“Mac Dolan offered to help me and… Yes, Mac Dolan.”

Mac slipped into the room, and Liv lifted her head. His gut clenched when he saw Misty settled in her lap behind the desk. The scene brought forth a tenderness he hadn’t felt in a long time, if ever. He did his best to squelch the squeamish feeling.

“Tempe,” she whispered, gripping her cell phone. “Everything’s going to be fine. I’ll call you back later.”

He moved farther into the room. “Problems at the Calloway ranch?” he asked.

Her lower lip trembled, but she straightened in her seat and lifted her chin. Mac felt much better until she explained. “I’m terrified that Mr. Kale will go after my family.”

TEN

She was doing her best to put on a strong front, but her chest felt so constricted she found it hard to breathe. What if Kale did go after her family? It would be her fault.

"Has anything happened at the Calloway ranch?" His brown eyes sharpened.

"Not yet, but that doesn't mean it won't."

"Did you tell her what's happening?" She nodded and Mac went on, "Then you've done all you can. She has Ewen there to help her. I'm sure they'll be fine." He abruptly changed the subject. "I have an associate looking into your email situation."

That got her attention. "What do you mean?" she asked in a sharp tone.

"I want to see if we can trace whoever placed that email in your Sent folder."

Mac's close scrutiny of her reaction to his statement made Liv feel as if she was under interrogation, and she didn't like it. She was usually the one making statements and watching for a person's reactions. She reminded herself Mac was pretty savvy, but how did he know someone with the technical skills to look into her email?

"Who?"

"Who what?"

"Who is it that you know with the proficiency to probe that deeply?"

Surprise briefly crossed his face, but it disappeared in an instant. "I made a few contacts in the military."

It was prevarication in its finest form. She studied his rugged face, searching for something—she didn't know quite what—but finally let it go. She needed all the help she could get, especially if Kale decided to go after Tempe, her new husband, Ewen, Tempe's daughter, Riley, and Aunt Effie. Not to mention all the other people on the Calloway ranch.

"Please keep me apprised." He gave a curt nod, and she moved on, saying wryly, "Don't be surprised if Tempe shows up even though I told her not to."

Leaning back on his boot heels, he grinned. "I like Tempe. She's one tough rancher, and she was a mighty fine Blue Angel. One of the best pilots the organization has ever seen, in my opinion."

She knew he wasn't comparing Liv to Tempe, but she couldn't help but do so herself. Tempe enjoyed the same lifestyle as Mac did, and to put it bluntly, Liv didn't.

"Yes, well, what's your opinion of our next step while we wait on… Who did you say was looking into my email?"

He glanced away—a sure sign he was getting ready to prevaricate. She'd seen it on many witnesses. But then he lifted his chin as if daring her to respond. "His online name is Spider."

For the first time that day, Liv choked out a laugh. "Spider? You're kidding, right? What's his real name?"

For the first time since Mac had rescued her on the side of the road, she saw a chink in that massive amount of confidence he had. His jaw squared. "I don't know his real name. He's an online contact who's done work for me before."

Liv jumped on that. "What kind of work?"

He waved a frustrated hand in the air. "That's not important. He'll come through. He always has in the past."

Liv was beginning to suspect there were many hidden facets to Mac beyond the slow-talking cowboy he presented to the world, but now was not the time to worry over that. She had to find a way to put Mr. Kale and his unsavory associates behind bars. It was no longer just about saving her career. Like Mac said after his plane burned to the ground, this was personal. Mr. Kale had crossed the line several times. Her Texas roots came to the fore, and Liv's mouth flattened in a grim line.

Before the conversation could digress, several voices floated up the stairs, and Barnie gave a bay of delight. At least she thought it was a bay of delight. It didn't have the same warning tone as his previous howls. Misty jumped off Liv's lap and tore out of the room.

"What now?" Mac asked before the words could leave Liv's mouth.

Pushing herself to her feet, she quickly moved toward the door, but Mac gently gripped her arm, stopping her from leaving the room. Their faces were so close, she picked up a pleasing spicy scent that swirled around him, causing her to lose focus for a few seconds.

"Liv, listen, you can trust me. I can help you, but

only if you've told me everything," he said in that slow, persuasive drawl of his.

The minute her brain processed his words, she jerked her arm away and took a step back, anger flaring so hot it made her shake. "You don't believe me, do you? You think I had something to do with Mr. Burton's death. How dare you pretend to want to help me." More words tumbled out of her mouth before she could stop herself. "How about this, cowboy—maybe *you* have an ulterior motive for helping *me*. Just maybe you're the one keeping secrets."

The moment the harsh accusation left her mouth, she regretted it. Mac had only offered to help her, and she wasn't being fair. As an attorney, she knew better than to make assumptions without proof.

Moving closer, she lifted her chin, willing him to see the truth in her eyes. "Mac, I apologize. My only excuse is that I'm on edge with everything that's happened in such a short period of time. I know you're only trying to help, and I appreciate everything you're doing. And to answer your question, I haven't withheld anything. Everything I've told you is the truth."

His face was a blank mask, and she couldn't read him. Had he accepted her apology? Not only did she have nowhere to turn, but deep down she couldn't stand the thought of him believing she meant the words she'd flung out in frustration and anger.

"There's only one thing I have to know," he said slowly, enunciating each word with care.

"Yes?" she asked, wondering what it could possibly be as he lowered his head and his mouth moved to within inches of hers. He suddenly jerked his head back and even took a step away before the blank mask on his face fell back into place.

"Forget what I said."

What did he have to know? The question screamed in Liv's mind, but it didn't matter. Her career, or what was left of it, was in New York, and Mac's life was on the ranch. Her thoughts must have been reflected in her expression, because he stepped back even farther.

Before she could respond a sharp, very familiar bark rose from downstairs. "Uh-oh."

"What?" Mac asked.

Liv grinned, adroitly ignoring the feeling that she'd lost something important. "You'll see." She paused. "Are we good?" she asked, knowing Mac understood what she meant.

"Yeah. Let's go see what all the ruckus is about."

Mac slowly followed Liv down the stairs, and the commotion in the foyer drew his attention. His head swiveled back and forth as he took in everything at once. It was all quite astonishing. Liv had her arms wrapped around a tall, full-figured, big-haired blonde woman who happened to be holding a solid white toy poodle in her arms. That in itself wasn't unusual. What left his mouth hanging open were the clothes both the woman and her dog were wearing. Never in his born days had he ever seen the likes of it.

Her tailored pink business suit, if it could be called a business suit, was studded with rhinestones around both the lapels and the hem of a skirt that flared just above her knees. The dog, if it was actually a dog, wore an outfit made out of the same material, and the rhinestones were attached to its collar. Patsy stood at the entrance to the kitchen wearing much the same expression he expected was on his own face. But the scariest part was Mac's brother. Fort stood to the side with a glazed expression. Mac had seen that look before when Fort thought himself in love, and it didn't bode well for the current situation.

Cal entered the foyer, Misty wrapped tightly in his arms, and moved straight toward Liv's friend when he spotted the poodle. Mac didn't see this ending well. He moved forward to intervene, but Cal reached the woman first. Liv had released her friend and stepped back, allowing a pathway for Cal to move in. Everyone froze when Cal—not as tall as Mac, but much more muscular and tough-looking—approached the big-haired woman wearing pink.

Mac admired the way Liv's friend stood her ground and stared back at Cal while he checked out the dog in her arms. Cal was the first to speak.

"German lines?"

Mac had no idea what Cal was talking about, but everyone watched with avid interest as the two rapid fired questions and answers at each other.

"Yes. Bred down from Cookie and Dominique."

"You compete in conformation?"

By now Liv's friend was grinning. "Yes."

"National or international?"

"We've placed in both."

Cal nodded and stepped back. Liv quickly jumped in. "Everyone, please meet my best friend from New York, Babette Chandler."

Mac moved in, extremely interested in Liv's best

friend. The company a person kept said a lot about them. "I'm Mac." He was caught off guard when Babette frowned at him.

"If you're trying to help Liv, as she told me on the phone, it might behoove you to check out the strange man I saw standing outside his car on the side of the highway right before I turned into your driveway," she said in a crisp northern accent, going right for his throat, to put it in canine terms.

Mac stiffened. "What, exactly, was he doing?"

Babette shrugged, her stiff hair moving with her shoulders. "I'm not quite sure. He was leaning against the side of his car. I just thought it strange that someone would be doing that here in the middle of nowhere."

Mac's thought whirled. If someone had enough money and power to buy and send in an armed drone, they could afford someone with the skills to hack into his security system and take it down long enough for a small army to slip onto the ranch. He needed more help to secure the ranch, and he needed it now.

Trying not to alarm anyone, he said, "Babette, it's nice to meet you, and you're right, I should look into that situation. If you'll excuse us, Fort and I will check the security system and make sure everything is up and running." He paused when Fort didn't move. "Fort!"

"Huh?" his brother responded, still staring at Babette.

Mac gritted his teeth. "Come with me. Now!"

Never taking his eyes off Babette, Fort followed. "Yeah, okay."

As upset as he was at the possibility of the ranch

being breached, Mac gave a half smile when Babette's voice floated down the hall behind them.

"Are all Texans that good-looking? Hey, doesn't that Fort guy play some sport or other? I've seen his advertisements all over social media. Is that his Lamborghini in the drive? It's too bad I crossed jocks off my dating list. Their travel schedules are horrendous, and they're too high-maintenance."

Liv snorted. "Wait until you meet Rex."

Fort slowed down—probably intending to interrupt the conversation—but Mac poked him in the back to get him moving.

"Stop that," Fort complained.

Mac punched in the code, and the door leading to the basement opened, then closed behind the two men. Mac took the stairs two at a time. He slid into his big leather chair and tapped several keys. His computer screen flared to life.

"There's no good reason for Liv's friend not to date me because I'm a baseball player," Fort grumbled.

Mac intently searched different quadrants of the ranch on the screens. "I thought you wanted to go out with Charlene?"

A chair squeaked across the floor as Fort pulled it beside Mac, then his brother slumped into it with the air of a doomed man. "I might as well give up on Charlene. She'll never go out with me."

Mac changed cameras, searching each quadrant of the ranch carefully. "And how hard have you tried?"

"Huh?"

At the end of his patience, with worry over Olivia

riding him hard, Mac swiveled his chair around and faced his brother. "You know what I think? Everything has always come easy for you. You went from all-star college athlete straight to the big time. I know you work hard at the sport, but you've never had to work hard at anything else. Everything, including dating women, has always been easy. Maybe you should think about that."

Fort's downcast look caused Mac to back off. All his brothers consistently came to him with their problems, and most of the time he didn't mind, but it was different now. That thought caused him to mentally rear back. Liv being here shouldn't make any difference, but somehow it did.

Fort straightened in his chair, and curiosity brightened his expression. "You're right," he said, a gleam in his eye that Mac didn't trust for a second. "I should think about that, and you have a lot on your plate right now, what with Liv Calloway and everything."

Mac stiffened. "Don't even go there. I'll not have my brothers playing matchmaker." Because Mac knew if Fort got something in his head, he'd be on the phone with all their brothers, and they'd gang up against him if they thought it was for his own good.

"Hey," Fort said unexpectedly, tumbling Mac from his morose thoughts and pointing at a screen behind him. "What's happening outside? Looks like they were getting her luggage out of the car."

Mac whipped around in his chair, saw what was happening and frantically hit a key, turning up the sound on the driveway cam. Both Liv and Babette were sprawled on the ground near the car with Babette underneath

Cal. What sounded like the ping of a bullet hitting the metal of the car sent Mac flying from his chair and out of the room.

ELEVEN

Her shoulder pounding in pain after being pushed to the ground by Cal, Liv struggled to gather her scattered thoughts. One second Babette had been grilling Liv about everything that had happened since Liv left New York, and the next second she'd heard a ping as something hit metal. Cal, who had accompanied them outside to help with Babette's massive amount of luggage, had plowed into both of them, knocking them to the ground. Liv had fallen sideways and hit the hard-packed dirt with her right shoulder. Now she lay there, pain piercing her arm and racing to her neck and spine.

Had someone shot at them? That's what it sounded like. Slowly rolling onto her back, she turned her head to the left, and what she saw had her forcing herself to her knees. Babette was trapped under the huge muscle mass of an unconscious Cal and struggling to get free.

"Liv, I can't breathe. Get this man off me."

A second shot pinged the car, this time only inches from Liv's head, and she dropped back to the ground. Someone was trying to kill her, and they'd come mighty close that time. Too close.

"I'm coming," Liv said, but the words came out as a whisper. "We have to get to the other side of the car. Someone is still shooting at us."

Taking another deep breath, she worked past the pain and belly crawled to Babette's side, staying as close to the vehicle as she could. Reaching over Cal's wide back, she pulled him halfway off her friend and scooted around them to the other side.

"Babette, we have to get to the other side of the car for cover. The shooter is on this side."

Her friend's eyes were large with fear, but she nodded and, with Liv's help, pulled herself out from under Cal. "What about Cal?" Babette asked.

Liv didn't answer until they had rounded the car, both of them on their knees. "They weren't aiming for Cal. It's me they want dead."

About that time Mac and Fort stealthily came zigzagging down the steps and across the driveway, both of them with rifles at the ready. Liv's heart thudded in relief and something else. This wasn't the first time Mac had risked his life to save hers, and it put a small crack in the protective shield she'd erected around her heart.

He rushed to her side and immediately looked at the blood on Babette's clothes. "Is she hit?" he asked crisply, as if holding any emotion at bay until they were safe.

"It's Cal's blood. Mac, you have to help him."

"Fort's taking care of Cal." The words were barely out of his mouth before he jumped up and followed Fort, protecting him while he carried Cal in a fireman's hold, thrown over his shoulder.

Watching every step they took, Liv held her breath

until they were safely through the front door, but took a short gasp when Mac came back for them. He took precautions the same as before, zigzagging as he ran, but she still held her breath until he was safely at her side.

"Liv, you and Babette go in front of me. I'll make sure nothing happens to you."

She nodded and grabbed Babette's hand. They got to their feet and waited for the go signal from Mac and then started running. Liv heard another shot and then return fire before they made it through the front door. Had Mac been hit? She'd never forgive herself if anything happened to him. When he came running through the opening and slammed the front door behind him, she released a huge breath.

"Are you okay?" he asked.

She nodded, then remembered to speak. "I'll probably be bruised, but I'm fine."

Mac looked over her shoulder at Fort. "Call Doc Hathaway. Tell him to get here as soon as possible."

Fort left to call the doctor, and Liv jerked her head toward Cal. He groaned, then attempted to push himself into a sitting position, finally achieving his goal and holding his right arm. Blood oozed thorough his fingers. Swinging her gaze back to Mac, she whispered, "How did this happen?"

"That man Babette spotted on the side of the road?"

"Yes."

"The ranch security was breached."

Grabbing Liv's arm, Babette breathed, "Liv, we could have been killed. Cal saved our lives. He's a hero."

Babette had always been rather dramatic, but she was right this time. "Yes, he did." Liv closed her eyes.

The sight of Babette covered in blood would stay with her the rest of her life. Flicking her eyes back open, she said, "Listen, Babette, I love you like a sister, and I can't tell you how much it means to me that you came all the way to Texas, but you have to go back to New York. It's too dangerous for you here."

Intelligent green eyes studied her for a long moment. "If your nasty boss is after you, who's to say he won't go after me in the city in order to get to you?"

Liv had to admit that Babette might be right.

"What about your businesses?" Liv asked.

Babette was proud to be the outcast of a wealthy New York clan due to the fact that she'd refused to marry the man they picked out for her, instead opting to go into the dog-grooming business. She owned three upscale stores in different parts of the city. It frustrated her family that most of their wealthy friends took their dogs to Babette's grooming facilities. Babette had guts, and Liv admired her greatly. The outlandish clothes her friend wore were in part a rebellion against her staunch, uptight family. Liv always thought Babette should have been born in the South, based on her flamboyant taste.

Before Liv had a chance to respond, she noticed Patsy standing pasty-faced in the arch between the foyer and kitchen.

"I heard shots. What happened?" Patsy asked, watching Mac and Fort help Cal up the stairs.

Liv hesitated, because Patsy might want her to leave after this incident, and Liv really did like Patsy. Any of the Dolans could have gotten shot in Cal's stead, and Liv had no doubt that Patsy, who loved the Dolan boys like a mother, would never have forgiven her.

Patsy touched her arm. "Tell me."

Choking out the words because she could still hardly believe it herself, Liv said, "Someone just tried to kill me, and Cal took a bullet to save our lives."

Patsy just nodded. "Let's see to the patient," she said, and Liv and Babette followed her up the stairs into a guest bedroom.

Patsy immediately started drilling out orders. "Liv, get a set of extra sheets from the hall closet. The ones on the top shelf. Babette, the washcloths are in there, too. Wet several and bring them to me."

Liv and Babette didn't move fast enough, so Patsy placed both hands on her hips. "This is a ranch, and accidents happen. I know what I'm doing."

Both women moved quickly to do as they were told. By the time Liv returned with the sheets, Mac and Cal were in the room. Cal groaned and Liv rushed forward. Patsy had already stripped the bed, so Liv and Patsy quickly spread the sheets on the mattress.

Mac grunted as he helped Cal, as gently as possible, onto the bed. When Cal was settled, Mac grabbed Liv's hand and tugged her into the hallway while Patsy went to work cleaning Cal up and Babette stood there watching.

"Are you really okay? I was afraid I would be too late when I realized there were bullets flying."

Liv stared into his concerned eyes, and something went all mushy inside her. She touched the side of his face and started to assure him she was fine, but then his words registered. "What do you mean, you almost didn't get there in time? How did you know someone was shooting at us if you were in the house?"

He grimaced, then shrugged and took her hand, leading her toward the stairs. "I heard them. Let's go to the basement where the security room is."

The brief feeling of connection with Mac was severed quickly as she allowed him to lead her to the basement. Just what did Mac have up his sleeve that she didn't know about?

What did it matter if she saw his computer room? He'd already told her he was a financial planner and that's how he was able to afford things. And it was true. She'd never know he contracted out with the FBI and had actually been hired to investigate her.

As he stopped at the hall and punched his code in, he could almost feel the curiosity coming off her in waves from close behind him. The door swung open, and he flicked on the light. She was hard on his heels as he descended the steps.

He moved toward his chair behind the large computer area before he realized she wasn't behind him and glanced back. She stood at the base of the stairs, her eyes rounded as she stared at the multiple screens mounted in a half circle around his desk.

"Well, you did say you were a financial planner," she said wryly, "but isn't this a little overkill?"

"Come over here," he said gruffly. "I'll show you the ranch's security system."

She winced in pain as she crossed the room, and Mac's natural protective instinct flared to life, but he doused it immediately. He had a job to do, he reminded himself, and it didn't include anything personal.

She pushed the extra chair close to the desk and

waited primly with her hands folded in her lap. Mac grinned before sitting, turning to his keyboard and pushing a few buttons. Even after the harrowing experience of being shot at, Liv Calloway still maintained perfect decorum. He admired her fortitude more than he was willing to admit. She was one tough lady, in his opinion.

The security cams went live, revealing all quadrants of the ranch. Everything was clear at the moment.

She leaned forward, studying the screens. "This is quite a system for a ranch out in the middle of Texas."

The lady was smart as a whip, and Mac knew he'd have to tread carefully. "After some of the things I saw in the military, well, let's just say I like to be careful."

It was time to ask more questions. "Liv, this thing you're in the middle of, there have to be some major players involved. Is there anything you can think of, anything at all, that will help us find evidence against your boss or his associates?"

"The big man never seems to be around when I need Him," she half mumbled under her breath.

"Are you talking about God?" Mac asked, surprised at the sudden change of subject. She appeared so dejected, he wanted to reach out and hug her, but he restrained himself. Gauging her response, you'd think he had thrown gasoline on a lit fire.

"I don't believe in God anymore," she exclaimed heatedly. "He took my parents when I needed them most, leaving me with a ton of responsibility, and then Grandpa died. I've worked my whole life to get where I am, and now my corrupt boss is destroying everything." She clamped her mouth shut, then sighed heavily. "I apologize for that outburst. I suppose it's been building for years." She dipped her chin, then gazed at him. "I suppose you're a believer?"

"Sure am. But, Liv, it seems to me that you have to believe in God in order to be angry at Him."

She sent him a sharp look, and Mac decided it was time to move on. "Let's get back to your situation. Outside of Mr. Burton, Mr. Stevenson, Murat Akin and Mr. Kale, do you know of any other players involved in the case you were working on?"

Mac couldn't help but notice the pretty little line of furrows that creased her brow when she went deep in thought. Her skin was smooth as silk, and she had the brightest smile he'd ever seen—when she smiled, that was, which hadn't happened but a time or two since she'd been at the ranch. Even her hands and fingers were elegant. He spotted two broken nails and frowned, briefly wondering if that had happened on the side of the road with the two thugs, or when she'd been shot at. For some reason, those broken nails didn't sit well with him. But it was her courage and grit that impressed him much more than her looks. A lot of people wouldn't have the guts to dig in and make sure justice was served.

"No," she said, heaving out a frustrated sigh, "I can't think of anyone else involved."

Mac snapped his mind back to business. "The firm is called Kale, Kale & Johnston. Were either of the other partners involved?" Liv shuddered, and Mac wondered what had caused that.

"It's my opinion that Mr. Johnston doesn't know half of what goes on at the firm. He's responsible for bringing in the moneyed clients rather than handling the actual cases. And Kale Jr. is Mr. Kale's son. To put it nicely, he's not as savvy as his father. I don't think he'd come up with a plan this elaborate to get rid of me."

Mac heard something in her voice. "Rode his daddy's coattails into the firm, did he?"

"No question, and I seriously doubt he has a clue about what's going on."

His computer pinged, and he swiveled his chair around to face the screens. They both watched as the cameras followed Doc Hathaway driving through the gate. He turned back to her. "Let's go see what the doctor has to say about Cal."

Liv rose stiffly before straightening her shirt.

"Are you sure you're okay?"

A grim, determined smile curved her lips. "I've taken tumbles off a horse that were worse than this. There'll be bruising, but I'll be fine."

Mac nodded. She was tough, but he'd do well to remember that she was all city now, no matter where she'd grown up.

After they checked on Cal, Mac planned to hire men to guard the ranch, and then he and Barnie were going hunting, except not for four-legged game. He considered bringing in the FBI for protection, but he wasn't ready to reveal his connection with the agency to Liv. And since Cal was injured and Mac would rather Fort not get hurt, hiring some men seemed to be the logical choice for the moment.

They both turned toward the stairs but stopped when a loud ping came from his computer.

"That's just a notification of an incoming email. I'll check it later." He moved toward the stairs. With everything he had going on, he really didn't want Liv to see whoever the email was from because it could be something from the FBI, but she didn't walk with him. She stood there and stared at his computer, then shot him a challenging look.

"Didn't you tell me you had someone named Spider checking into the intrusion of my email? That might be them."

Yep, the woman was one smart cookie, but just how smart was she? Did she want to stick around and see if Spider had found out that she actually did send that email? And if she was innocent? Maybe she wanted to see if Spider had unearthed any information. Either way, this might be a good time to gauge her reaction if the email was indeed from Spider.

He blocked the computer screen until he noted the sender, then he moved to the side.

"Well, now," he drawled, "it looks like Spider's been busy." He held his breath when he opened the message. This could prove Liv's guilt or innocence, and he found he really wanted her to be innocent. It was short and to the point.

Hey, man. I did find where someone hacked into your little chickie's computer, but I need to dig deeper. Hackers are in and out of computers all the time. I'll keep looking and be in touch.

The email disappeared within seconds.

Her brows snapped together. "That email disappeared just like the text Mr. Kale sent me." She studied him for a long moment, then asked slowly, "Just who are you, Mac Dolan?"

Another alert sounded in the room, and Mac tensed. After he hit a few computer keys, one screen revealed several men dressed in black sneaking onto the property.

TWELVE

Mac and Liv left the basement and hurried down the hall just as Patsy opened the door for Doc Hathaway. According to Tempe, who had kept Liv in the loop during her time away, the retired and renowned cardiac surgeon had moved to Texas after his wife died, and everyone in the area called on him because he was the closest available doctor. He was a big believer in church and community and always helped when asked.

Liv skidded to a stop when Mac came to a sudden halt in front of her.

"Patsy, take Doc Hathaway upstairs. There's a matter I have to see to."

Liv couldn't see Mac's face, but she did note Patsy's immediate understanding that this was a serious matter. Liv jumped when Mac bellowed up the stairs.

"Barnie! Come!"

Barnie came charging down the stairs, ears flapping the whole way as he passed Patsy and the doctor on their way up. Grabbing his coat and Stetson off a coat rack, Mac opened the door and Liv went into action, seizing him by the back of his jacket.

"Stop!"

He peered over his shoulder, and Liv took a step back at the fierceness covering his face. His square jaw was locked, his lips formed a straight line and his eyes… They were lit with the call of battle. That was the only way to describe it.

"Where are you going?" She was proud of how strong her words came out.

"I'm going hunting," he said with a resoluteness that caused shivers to tap their way up her spine. She was seriously afraid he wasn't referring to hunting animals after seeing the men dressed in black on the security screen.

Squaring her own jaw, she shot back, "Not without me, you're not."

"You're staying here."

It was a drill-sergeant command, and Liv had never done very well with outright orders. "You're going after them, aren't you? The men who breached your security. I'm coming with you."

"No. You're. Not," he said through clenched teeth. "It's too dangerous."

Liv stood tall—well, as tall as her height would allow. "Mac, this is my battle. I'm coming whether you like it or not." He didn't back down, and she tried another tack. "If you leave, I'll just follow you."

He looked like he wanted to spit nails, but he gave her a curt nod. "Grab your jacket. We're going on horseback. I know this ranch like the back of my hand. If they're here, I'll find them."

Liv took her jacket off the coatrack and slipped it on before he could change his mind. Mac also grabbed

Barnie's K-9 vest on his way out the door. "Why do we need that?"

"It's best to be prepared" was Mac's curt response.

Liv was seeing a totally different man than the laid-back cowboy she'd come to know in such a short period of time. This Mac was on a mission, and nothing would stop him. What other facets of his personality did he keep hidden? Online friends with unusual capabilities. A successful financial planner. A retired Blue Angel. A cowboy. Yes, there was much more to Mac than initially met the eye, and she couldn't help but be drawn to him.

As they entered the large barn, Liv blinked several times to allow her eyes to adjust to the interior and was astounded when everything came into focus. When they were searching for Misty, she'd been too upset to pay attention to her surroundings. The place was a marvel. Mac must make quite a bit as a financial planner. The high ceiling and walls were made of polished pine, and attached to each stall door was a brass nameplate elegantly stating the horse's name. Six gorgeous horses hung their heads over the stalls, watching their every move.

The horse Mac approached threw his head back and snorted. Liv's breath caught at the beauty of the creature. If she wasn't mistaken, it was a stunning paint horse. The muzzle was solid white partway up the jaw with a black head. The rest of its body was painted black and white, as per the breed.

Mac, who had already moved into the stall, nodded at the one across the aisle. "I'm riding Thunder, and that's Molly. If you're coming with me, you'd best get her saddled."

Liv turned around and found herself face-to-face with the gentlest pair of brown eyes she'd ever seen. Her heart melted, and she was surprised to realize how much she'd missed riding. But there was no time to lose. She had no doubt that Mac would leave her behind if she didn't hurry.

Rubbing Molly's muzzle, she whispered calmly while saddling the brown-and-white paint. "That's a sweet girl, Molly. You and I are going to get along just fine."

She mounted Molly just as Mac rode out the front door of the barn, Barnie trotting at Thunder's side. Firming her resolve, she followed him out. This was her fight, and she didn't want Mac to get hurt. Shying away from examining her feelings too closely, she clicked the reins and moved Molly forward.

Mac never stopped scanning the horizon as they rode in silence for a while, seeing nothing but scrub brush and a few rocky hills spaced pretty far apart as they got closer to the foothills, which were standing guardian to the Chisos Mountains. She shivered, thinking about people who had gotten lost or stranded in those massive mountains over the years. Glancing at Barnie, she wondered if Mac had found any of those people.

Surprised when Mac brought Thunder to a standstill, Liv guided Molly alongside Thunder. "What is it?" she asked almost in a whisper. For all her brave talk, they were in the middle of nowhere and extremely exposed.

"I don't know. Something doesn't feel right."

"Please don't tell me it's another drone. I can live

the rest of my life without ever seeing another of those things, toy or not." Liv knew she was babbling, but she tended to talk when she got nervous. His mouth twitched just the tiniest bit, and his shoulders relaxed. She was glad she could be of service, but they were still sitting ducks, and Mac had just said something didn't feel right.

"Let's hope not."

Another, more unsettling thought occurred to her. "What happens if they do send another drone after us?"

He raised a dark brow. "I'll shoot it down like I did the last one."

"What doesn't feel right?" she asked, twisting around in her saddle to see if anything was out there.

"I don't know, I just—"

Barnie threw back his head and bayed loudly right before Liv heard a whistling sound and Mac dug his heels into Thunder's sides and yelled, "Go! Go! Go! Head for the mountains!"

Bouncing in the saddle, Mac glanced over his shoulder to check on Liv and held his breath when she was almost unseated as Molly took off after Thunder. Grabbing the reins, she leaned forward over the horse's neck as they galloped beside Mac and his stallion, Barnie running alongside them, trying his best to keep up. Liv held on as best as she could. Molly might be gentle, but the horse was fast.

Molly swerved sideways when another bullet hit the dirt near the horse's hooves, and Mac shifted to place himself and his horse between Liv and the line of fire.

They finally reached a large foothill, and Mac led

them around to the other side, giving them cover. As soon as the horses came to a stop, he jumped off Thunder and rushed to her side, Barnie panting heavily as he came up close to them.

"Are you okay? Did you get hit?"

It took a moment for her to catch her breath, but she shook her head, and he took that to mean she was okay. He stared at her a minute, then made a sharp pivot and pulled a rifle out of an encasing attached to Thunder's saddle. His word clipped and short, he said, "Stay here. I'm going to track that sharpshooter. He can't be more than three or four hundred yards away."

He turned to leave, but he should have known better. She slid off her horse and caught up with him. "Mac, no," she said. "I won't allow you to do this."

He whipped around, and she took a step back, away from the stone-cold vibes she felt rolling off him. In the blink of an eye, he relaxed himself and turned on the charm. Maybe that would keep her in place and safe. Placing both hands on her shoulders, he said, "Liv, we need to locate the people who breached the ranch's security, and it'll be dangerous. You'll be safe here."

Mac knew she'd just been through a harrowing experience, but he bristled when she said, "Don't pull that cowpoke routine on me. I'm not staying here hiding like a good little woman. I'm coming with you."

His charm disappeared as frustration ate at him. His jaw clenched so hard he heard his teeth grind. "Fine, but you have to promise to do what I tell you. If I say get down, you hit the ground as fast as you can."

She straightened her shoulders. "I'll do as you say, but what about the horses?"

"They'll stay put, and if we're gone too long, they'll find their way back to the barn. You have to stay right behind me. I'm going around behind where I think the shooter is positioned—if they're still there."

She nodded her agreement, but Mac knew he'd have to keep a close eye on her because the woman always seemed to walk right into the middle of flying bullets.

He took long strides forward with Barnie at his side, and Liv had to double step in order to stay close behind him. Could someone have her and Mac in their sights right now? In the courtroom, she had no lack of confidence, and even though she'd grown up on a ranch, she'd lived in the city for a long time. Sure, there were dangers in the city, but there were also more places to hide. She felt completely exposed out here in the middle of nowhere. They had just rounded the back side of another foothill when Mac came to a sudden stop, causing her to bump into him.

"Sorry," she mumbled, but she noticed he was staring up the back side of a hill. She squinted and searched until she finally noticed a very small piece of black material snagged on a bush. Up high.

He glanced at her and said, "Hang tight, I'm going to grab that."

She touched his arm. "Mac, I don't know, that's pretty steep."

He grinned, and her heart beat a little faster at the transformation. She decided she much preferred the laid-back Mac. His other persona actually intimidated her a bit, but she'd never, ever let him know it.

"Is that concern I hear in your voice, Miss Calloway?"

It was, maybe more than she was comfortable with. "I'd be concerned about anyone in this circumstance," she answered crisply.

His smile slipped away and she wanted to recapture her words, but it was too late. He placed the toe of one boot on a small ledge and pulled himself up. She practically held her breath the whole time he was climbing and only relaxed when he made his way back down, the piece of cloth encased in a hankie. After his feet were planted firmly on the hard Texas soil, he moved close to her.

"We both know you were worried about *me*, Liv," he said in that sure, confident manner of his that made her bristle. He leaned toward her, but she automatically took a step back. He froze in place, a mask of indifference falling over his face. Grabbing the K-9 vest he'd brought along, he slipped it onto Barnie. "I apologize for stepping into your boundaries. There's no excuse for that."

He made it sound as though she thought she was better than him, and that wasn't it at all. But before she could explain her career plans again, which didn't seem nearly as important as they did before she arrived in Texas, he held the black scrap of cloth under the hound's nose.

"Barnie. Find!" Barnie went into tracking mode, and it was obvious the dog was thrilled to get to work.

Liv had to harness her emotions about Mac, because there were more important things to worry about—like staying alive and salvaging her career. Liv's attention was drawn to Barnie as he sniffed around the base of the foothill for a minute or so, then took off with Mac right behind him.

"Get a move on, Liv," Mac yelled.

And she did. Thirty minutes later, she was wishing she'd worn tennis shoes instead of boots, and her shoulder was throbbing, but she gritted her teeth and kept moving. They wound their way around several foothills before Barnie led them out into the open. They were headed back toward the ranch house, and she noticed Mac picking up speed. Her heart stuttered at the thought of the person who shot at them going toward the house. Liv pictured Babette, Cal, Patsy, Fort and the ranch hands, any of whom could get hurt.

But just as the house came into view, Barnie, his nose to the ground, took a sharp right turn and headed toward a very small foothill a reassuring distance from the house. Liv bent over, trying to catch her breath while Mac watched Barnie with what she could only describe as a hunter's expression on his face.

Barnie took off again and ran at an angle that ended up parallel to the driveway leading out to the road. Liv dodged scrub brush as she got farther behind Mac and Barnie. Finally, unable to go any farther, she bent at the waist, gasping for breath. Working out at a gym, she thought grimly, certainly hadn't prepared her to run a marathon in cowboy boots.

She lifted her head from her bent-over position, and just as she almost lost sight of Barnie and Mac, Barnie made another sudden turn and headed back in her direction. Relief that she wouldn't have to follow them was almost overwhelming. She stood up straight, but suddenly something with enough force to knock her forward slammed into the back of her shoulder.

As she fell in what felt like slow motion, she saw Mac running toward her, yelling, and she couldn't quite make out what he was saying. But when pain exploded in her shoulder, she realized, with a moment of sudden clarity, that she'd been shot.

THIRTEEN

Mac forced himself to stay calm as he ran toward Liv, praying with every fiber of his being that she was alive. He had seen enough men shot while he was in the military to know what had happened to her. She had to be okay. He should never have allowed her to accompany him.

When he reached her, he fell to his knees and laid two fingers on the side of her neck. He took his first full breath after finding a strong, steady beat and immediately went into action. He didn't call Barnie off the hunt, hoping the dog would force the sniper to move out of position, giving them a chance to get back to the house. Mac's calmness under fire slipped away when he stared at the beautiful, petite woman lying crumpled on the ground. Hair had slipped from her ponytail, and dirt covered her jeans. This was his fault.

He touched her, and she groaned. "Liv, honey, we have to move. Barnie's gone after the sniper, so we should have a good chance of getting to the house." Another bullet whizzed past Mac, landing mere inches from Liv's head. He scooped her up and ran toward the trees close to them, taking them out of the sniper's sight.

He stopped and looked at Liv in his arms, startled to see her glaring at him.

"You let Barnie go after the shooter all by himself? Mac, I'll never forgive you if that dog gets hurt. He saved Misty and I haven't even given him his steak. If that shooter harms one hair on that dog, I'll make sure Mr. Kale spends the rest of his life in the worst prison in the country."

Mac quickly realized that Liv was handling the shock of what happened by ignoring the blood seeping through her shirt and focusing on Barnie. He held her closer, garnering her attention. "Listen, you've been shot in the shoulder. Can you walk or do I need to carry you? We have to get moving."

That statement paused her diatribe, and she jerked her gaze toward the nearest small foothill. "I-is he still out there?"

Barnie released a loud bay, and Mac grinned despite the terror still filling him when he saw Liv go down—something he'd have bad dreams about for years to come. "I think Barnie found what he was looking for." Not long after Barnie's signal, they heard a vehicle start up and tear down the highway.

"Come on, let's get you to the house. We're probably safe for the time being. Hopefully Doc Hathaway will still be there."

"I can walk," she said and wiggled, forcing him to release her and set her down.

Those big brown eyes, normally so full of vitality, were full of something else, something that made him want to pull her back into his arms and cherish and protect her forever. He shook that off when she grabbed his hand. She swayed, and he immediately wrapped an arm around her waist. "Come on, let's go."

They were quiet until about halfway to the house, when she pulled away from him. "I'm fine. I can make it now."

Mac felt her pull away emotionally as well as physically. He could almost visualize her building an invisible barrier between her and any possible relationship, all for her ten-year career plan. Fear for her life and his feeling of absolute helplessness when she got shot, along with the tumultuous emotions his failed marriage evoked, came bursting forth like a long-dormant geyser.

"Is it worth it?" The short question shot out of his mouth like a cannon blast, revealing way more than he intended, but it was too late to call it back.

"I don't know what you're talking about," she said, her expression telling him to back off, but he couldn't let it go, because when her body had jerked forward when that bullet hit her… Well, something inside him rebelled at the idea of Liv not being around.

"Giving up everything for your career. Is it worth it?"

She slowed her steps and swayed slightly. Feeling like the worst kind of heel for questioning her while she was injured, Mac wrapped his arm around her waist again, and they moved forward.

"I apologize. I was out of line."

"She did a real number on you, didn't she?" Liv asked. It was more of a statement than a question, and he knew what she was referring to. For the first time since his divorce, the words just tumbled out of his mouth.

"I'm partially to blame. She said she wanted a family, but we didn't really discuss a timeline before we walked down the aisle. When her career took off, she finally admitted she didn't know if she ever wanted children." He paused, remembering words thrown out in the heat of the moment that couldn't ever be taken back. "After I finished my time with the Blue Angels, I mustered out and was ready to start a family. I grew up in a large family and wanted to create my own. That's when things went south."

"I'm sorry things didn't work out, Mac. But I want you to know, you're a noble and courageous man. You'll get your family one day."

Before he could respond to what amounted to a brush-off, the house came into view, and they were interrupted by a very angry woman stomping from the driveway toward them with a well-dressed, seemingly amused man following in her wake. Tempe Calloway, now Tempe Duncan, stopped short in front of them and propped her fists on slim hips, taking in the scene in a glance.

She addressed her sister first. "Liv, you okay?"

Liv smiled, and it was genuine. "I will be as soon as I see Doc Hathaway."

Tempe turned her wrath on Mac. "I come over to check on my sister only to find her bleeding?"

Mac had flown in the Blue Angels with Tempe, and he liked her, but she raised his hackles with her insinuations. "It was Liv's choice to stay here."

Tempe cast her gaze back and forth between Mac and Liv, and her eyes flickered, as if she'd come to some kind of conclusion known only to her. Mac would like to know what it was, because he could sure use some enlightenment right about now. But first things first.

"Let's take it inside. A sniper shot Liv. I think he left, but I'll feel better indoors."

Standing beside him, Liv suddenly gasped and grabbed his arm. "Barnie! Where is he?"

Tempe pulled her sister away and glared at Mac. "Go find your dog. We're going inside."

No sooner were the words out of Tempe's mouth than Barnie came tearing around the corner of the barn, slobber dripping from his mouth. Mac watched as Liv dropped to her knees and enveloped Barnie in a big hug. His dog licked her all over the face, and Mac's heart melted like butter when the city gal didn't even try and stop him. It melted even more when she praised Barnie for doing such a good job. He didn't realize Tempe had come up beside him until he felt her bony elbow connect with his ribs.

"Liv told me about her boss, but what else is going on with my sister?"

Mac didn't want to talk to Liv's ornery sister. He felt as if he'd taken a punch to the gut watching Liv on her knees in the dirt loving on Barnie, and he needed some space to think things through.

"You'll have to ask her. Get everyone inside. I think the threat is gone for the moment, but you never can tell."

The horses came stampeding in and headed for the barn, just as he knew they would, so that was one less thing Mac had to worry about.

Tempe threw one last salvo. "Mac, you break my sister's heart, I'll be paying you a private visit."

And with that threat left hanging in the air, Tempe

helped Liv to her feet and the group headed toward the house, Barnie following in their wake.

Tempe stayed close to Liv as they climbed the front steps and walked through the door leading into the house. Liv braced herself.

"First, we're going to find Doc Hathaway so he can take a look at you, then you're going to tell me why Doc's here in the first place. You told me everything about Mr. Kale, but you haven't called and kept me updated on what's going on here at the ranch."

As they moved through the foyer, Liv felt like a heel. "I'm sorry. Everything has been happening so fast, and I didn't want to worry you. None of this is Mac's fault. He's only been trying to help me."

Tempe looked at her kind of funny, then broke out in a grin, making Liv wonder what that was all about. "Okay, let's get Doc Hathaway to clean you up, then we'll have a chat."

Liv was too weary to argue, so she just led the way up the stairs. Tempe followed her into the room where they'd placed Cal, and her sister exclaimed, "What in the world's going on around here?"

Liv glanced at the situation in the room and completely understood Tempe's dismay. Doc Hathaway was placing a dressing on Cal's arm wound. Babette was fussing over the man, fluffing his pillows. Misty and Boots, Babette's dog, were curled up against the large man's side, and Patsy was putting a tray beside the bed that held a snack and what looked like tea. Barnie completed the picture by sauntering in and plopping his bottom on the floor, whining at the two tiny female dogs lying on the bed with the patient. Fort was the only one missing.

The whole thing struck Liv as funny, and she started laughing, except it came out more hysterical than humorous. To think, this time last week, except for her misgivings about the firm she worked for, her life had been perfectly normal and her career plan was on schedule.

Doc Hathaway finished with Cal and came over to her, concern written on his face as he stared at the blood seeping through her fingers. "That's two gunshot wounds now. Have you called the sheriff?"

"No!" The word escaped before Liv could stop it. She rubbed her temple with her right hand. "Sorry. I'm just..." She swayed, and Doc Hathaway led her to a chair, pulling her arm out of her shirtsleeve so he could examine where the bullet went in. Liv tensed as he poked and prodded on the back of her upper shoulder, then on the front.

"Well, young lady, you're fortunate. The bullet went in and came out the other side. It's a flesh wound, but I need to clean it well. You should go to a hospital, and so should the man on the bed."

No way was she going to a hospital, where they had to report gunshot wounds. "Just clean it up. I'll be okay." It throbbed, but she'd take some ibuprofen. She winced when he put some kind of antiseptic on it that burned like fire.

Liv briefly wondered where Mac was, but one look at Tempe's face and she knew she'd be tied up for a while answering her sister's questions. After the doctor was finished, Liv thanked him and motioned Tempe out of the room. Neither one said a word until they were in Liv's bedroom. Tempe's boot heels clicked with every step as she paced the floor while Liv took a seat in one of the chairs, making herself comfortable. She waited and was flabbergasted when Tempe fired her first question—not the one Liv had expected.

"What's going on with you and Mac?"

"What?"

Tempe stopped right in front of her. "What's going on with you and Mac? It's not that I don't like the guy. I do. It's just that I know he went through a nasty divorce and I don't want you hurt."

Liv shook her head. "It's not like that. He offered to help me, that's all."

Tempe studied her for a moment, as if trying to read her mind, but said, "Okay, you told me about your boss, but I want to know everything that's been going on around here. And I mean everything, Liv. Don't leave anything out."

Liv took a deep breath and started from the time Mac saved her from the kidnappers on the side of the road. Tempe's face hardened when she heard about that. When Liv got to the drone part, her sister's face went pasty white, then flushed red with anger.

"And one of the drones shot Mac's plane, and it burned to the ground."

Tempe tilted her chin. "The Cessna," she breathed. Tempe loved to fly, having been a Blue Angel herself, and the idea of the plane meeting its demise obviously struck a chord with her. Especially since she and Ewen had almost been killed in it after they borrowed it from Mac when someone was after Tempe.

"Go on."

Liv slumped in her chair. "I can't believe I've become dependent on one of the rowdy Dolan boys. Don't get me wrong, Mac has risked his life several times to save mine, but I'm used to fending for myself."

Tempe snorted. "Mac left his childhood behind a long time ago. The man's smart as a whip. Only the best and brightest become Blue Angels, and everyone in the unit asked his advice on investments. Plus, he not only remodeled his parents' house, but he's building his own home on another part of the ranch."

Liv's head snapped up. "He's building a house?"

Tempe studied her for the longest time, then moved on, and Liv was relieved.

"What are you doing to prove your innocence and bring down your boss? You know Ewen has some major connections. What can we do to help?"

"Go home and tell Ewen to hire extra security until this is over. I'll handle things here," Mac said from the doorway. Liv hadn't even heard him approach.

"Are you gonna use your own resources?" Tempe's eyes narrowed, and she added mysteriously, "Or are those resources the reason you're involved in this?"

Mac folded his arms across his chest. "And what might you know about my resources?"

"I know a lot of things. Don't forget I married a man with many, many connections."

Liv watched both of them, trying to figure out what they were referring to. It was as if they were having a coded conversation. "What are you two talking about?"

Tempe and Mac stared at each other for the longest time, but Liv knew when her sister made a decision, because she gave a sharp nod to Mac and turned toward Liv without answering her question. "Will you come to the ranch with me and let us help you with this?"

Liv was adamant. "No. I refuse to risk my niece or any of you. This is my problem, and I'll deal with it."

Mac chimed in. "Plenty of security is on the way as we speak. I called them while the doc was patching you up."

Tempe looked back and forth between them again, then faced Liv. "I want your word that you'll keep me posted on everything going on here."

Liv sighed a breath of relief. "I promise."

Tempe pivoted on her boot heel and faced Mac. "You let anything happen to my sister, you'll answer to me."

"Yes, ma'am," he drawled in that deceptively slow accent of his Liv had come to recognize he used as a buffer, hiding his true thoughts and feelings.

Liv stood and hugged her sister goodbye, then waited until Tempe's footsteps receded down the hallway before facing down Mac.

"What were you and Tempe talking about?" she asked.

Liv shrugged. "I brought her up to speed on everything that's been happening."

He moved closer, and although the tic in his jaw indicated high emotion, his brown eyes were warm and full of concern.

"You were shot," he said gruffly.

Liv read the emotion behind his husky words. It sounded like he really cared about her, and she found herself hoping that was the case. But he stepped away when she didn't respond, and that was probably for the best.

"I'll be okay." Her response came out sounding pathetically weak, and she cleared her throat, grappling for something to say to fill the uncomfortable void. "You said you hired some security?"

He gave a curt nod. "They'll be here tonight," he said, his dark brown eyes alert and studying her intently. She had the oddest feeling he was expecting something from her, but she was clueless as to what. He left the room as quietly as he entered, and Liv slumped back into the chair. Her shoulder throbbed, and she laid her head back, closed her eyes and let her thoughts drift until the odd conversation between Mac and Tempe snagged in her mind.

She mulled it over the way she did a witness's testimony. Tempe knew something about Mac that Liv didn't, but why wouldn't her sister tell her? She should have challenged that during the conversation, but she blamed her lack of clarity and weak resolve on exhaustion and her life having been turned upside down.

She'd always felt Mac was holding something back, and she was determined to find out what he was hiding.

FOURTEEN

Mac took the stairs two at a time, wondering what was wrong with him. He couldn't seem to keep his mind off Liv. He admired her courage and strength in the face of everything being thrown at her. She was an amazing woman—braver than a lot of men he knew, especially for such a dainty lady. She was also smart and beautiful and tough, but she wasn't for him. He might be ready to settle down and have babies, but it would have to be with the right woman.

In the foyer, he took a sharp right into the kitchen, where Patsy was busy starting dinner. He grabbed an apple out of a basket sitting on the table and bit into the juicy fruit harder than intended because he was disgusted with himself. He had to stay focused on proving Liv's innocence or guilt. Until that happened, it didn't matter what he thought.

"I've been hankering for some pork chops. They smell good," he said, just to make conversation.

Patsy whipped around and gave him the stink eye. "I was passing Liv's bedroom and saw you standing real close to her, like you were going to kiss her. I'll not have you breaking that girl's heart."

That didn't sit well. "Me break her heart? You ever think about her breaking mine?" Mac wanted to stuff the words back into his mouth as soon as they escaped, but it was too late. The contemplative expression shining out of his housekeeper's eyes said it all. Instead of trying to backpedal, he took option number two and left the room. He was headed toward the front door with the intent of escaping outside when he heard the sound of Liv's voice drifting from the living room. She must have come downstairs while he was in the kitchen.

Like a moth closing in on a roaring flame, he eased back down the hallway, drawn to her. He stopped short when he heard Fort's voice and rolled his eyes when he caught the gist of the conversation.

"But, Liv, Charlene is a bookworm, and she doesn't even like baseball. I've asked her out several times, and she just shakes her head like I don't get it. I don't understand what she wants from me. All I want to do is take her on a date."

Intrigued, Mac leaned against the wall just outside the door, interested to see just how Miss Career Woman would respond to Fort's plea.

"Charlene sounds like a woman I'd like, Fort."

"Why is that?" his befuddled brother responded, and Mac could visualize him scratching his head.

"Well," Liv said in a much softer voice than she'd ever used on Mac, "because she sounds like she has principles."

"That's all well and good, but how do I get her to go out with me?"

Mac grinned. Fort was like a tick on a dog when he wanted something.

"What types of things does she enjoy doing?"

"Huh?" was his brother's brilliant response.

"You know, does she enjoy the theater, going to the movies? Things like that."

"Well, she likes to read. She's a librarian, you know."

The room went quiet, and Mac caught himself leaning farther toward the door, wondering what Liv would come up with.

"Why don't you ask her what she's reading, then go buy the book and read it so you can discuss it with her?"

Fort grunted, and Liv went on with an exasperated tone. "Fort, you need to find out what she's interested in and involve yourself in her life."

Mac got a warm, fuzzy feeling at the thought of Liv helping one of his brothers—especially Fort, because he was enough to try anyone's patience. He'd just started moving toward the open doorway, deciding it was high time to rescue Liv, when the front doorbell rang.

Automatically going into warrior mode, Mac bent over and pulled out the small pistol strapped to his calf as he headed to the front door. He'd set up the security system to go full-scale alert if anyone breached the perimeters, but there was a softer, short alert if anyone came down the driveway. Neither one had sounded. Whoever was ringing his doorbell had bypassed everything, and that didn't bode well.

Patsy came out of the kitchen, wiping her hands on a towel, and her eyes widened when he motioned her back with the gun in his hand. She disappeared, and Mac casually dropped his arm to his side before he glanced through the small square glass at eye level on the door. He didn't see a gun in the guy's hand, but that didn't mean his visitor wasn't packing. With his pistol hanging loosely at his side, he cracked the door just wide enough to identify the visitor or intruder—whichever it turned out to be. He could always slam the door shut, and the wood was thick enough to stop a bullet if necessary.

His finger on the trigger of his pistol, he gazed out and was shocked to find a skinny guy with dark, unkempt hair and too many rings in his ears to count. Mac took in everything at a glance. The guy appeared to be in his early twenties, and he stood there fidgeting and glancing over his shoulder, as if someone was after him. Mac peered down the driveway but didn't see anyone. The only thing there was an old rattletrap of a car squatting in the driveway.

"Who are you and how did you get onto my property? And you better answer fast."

The guy finally stopped fidgeting and lifted his chin. "It's your fault that I'm here."

Mac relaxed his body, but inside he was drawn tight as a drum. "And how's that?" he asked casually.

The beanpole grinned and held out an elegant hand that was in complete contrast to the rest of his body. "You know me as Spider."

Mac stiffened. "And how do I know you're who you say you are?"

The guy did another head check behind him. "You hired me to look into the Liv Calloway problem. C'mon, man, let me in. It's not safe out here."

Mac opened the door, and Spider's eyes widened when he saw the pistol in Mac's hand, but then a big grin split his face. "Dude, I sure made the right choice coming here."

Mac's fingers tightened on the pistol. He'd never met Spider, didn't even know his real name. This could be someone hired by Liv's boss for all he knew. "Talk and talk fast. Why are you here?"

"You hired me to find out if someone placed that email in Liv Calloway's Sent box," he said quickly. "I'm still digging, but somewhere along the way, somebody must've realized what I was doing and started tracking me." He shivered. "Next thing I know, somebody trashed my place while I was out and stole my computer." He grinned again, patting the side of the backpack he was carrying. "But I never leave my main computer at home. It goes everywhere I go.

"There was nothing else I was working on that would have prompted someone breaking into my place, so I figured it was related to Liv Calloway. Anyway, after doing a little research and finding out you live here in the middle of nowhere, I figured this place was as safe as anywhere in the city, even though your security has been breached several times—which I can help shore up, by the way."

Mac arched a brow, and Spider started talking faster. "Anyway, I figured you owed me, seeing as how you're partly responsible for those dudes coming after me."

"And you bypassed my security system to get in?"

"Yeah, and man, you really should do something about that system. It's high-tech, but I can fix it so that only the highest-caliber hackers can get in."

Mac finally relaxed. Not about the fact that people could hack into his expensive security system, but because the more Spider talked, the more he sounded like his online personality. Spider's eyes widened as he peered behind Mac.

"Wow, man, is that, like, Fort Dolan, the baseball player?" His gaze jerked back to Mac. "I didn't do a search on your family."

Mac snorted. "No, you just hacked into my security system and decided to show up for an uninvited visit."

Spider shrugged his thin shoulders, and Mac wanted to smack him.

"Just curious, man."

Fort and Liv approached, and Liv tentatively asked, "A friend of yours, Mac?"

Mac closed his eyes for a second or two before opening them. It felt like his house was turning into a hotel, but when he saw the questioning, somewhat fearful look in Liv's eyes, he knew why he was doing this. Yes, he'd been contracted by the FBI to find out the truth about Liv Calloway, but the longer he was around her, well, his mission was changing.

"Liv, this is Spider."

Fort made a strangling noise that sounded a lot like laughter, but Liv surprised Mac when she rushed forward and enveloped Spider in a big hug. Something that felt an awful lot like jealousy coursed through him as he watched Liv wrap her arms around the beanpole. She was beaming when she pulled back.

"I can't thank you enough for helping Mac look into my problem."

Spider beamed. "Happy to help. I'm still working on it."

Before Mac could break up the mutual admiration fest, the security system started shrieking.

* * *

Liv tensed when the alarm went off, half expecting a drone to shoot a miniature rocket through a window. Mac opened the closet door in the foyer, tucking his pistol back on his person and pulling out a much larger gun, which prompted her into action.

"What are you doing?" She took a step back when he faced her. His eyes were frozen slits of granite, and the sharp angle of his jaw didn't bode well for his enemy.

"I'm going on the defensive. I'm tired of playing their game. Someone's going to get hurt."

His words scared her so bad that each thump of her heart pounded in both her ears. "Mac, you can't do this. They have drones and sharpshooters." She took a deep breath, straightened her shoulders and called up her years of training in the courtroom. "I won't have you getting hurt because of me."

And like the flip of a light switch, he morphed into the laid-back cowboy he presented to the world. "You worried about me, Liv?"

She almost made a flippant retort but hesitated. His question was asked casually, but it didn't quite make the mark. There was real curiosity behind the query. "Of course, I'm worried" was all she could think to say. He gave a short nod and turned to open the front door.

"Wait," she said, feeling as if she hadn't given him what he was looking for, but how could she when she was confused herself? "What are you going to do?"

"I'm going to find those guys."

"How?" she snapped without meaning to because, well, she couldn't imagine a world without Mac in it.

"I'm flying over the ranch to see if I can locate them. None of us are safe until they're gone."

Liv nudged him out of the way and grabbed her jacket out of the closet.

"What're you doing?"

With the same determination she used against hostile jurors, she faced him down. "I'm coming with you."

"No!"

"Yes! This is my fight, and I'm coming."

"You just got shot. You're in no condition to come."

"He's got a point," Fort drawled from somewhere behind her.

She'd forgotten he was there but whirled around and directed her wrathful fear toward him. "Why don't you go find a book to read?"

He held up his hands in surrender. "Just saying."

Spider stayed off to the side, watching in wide-eyed wonder, but Liv wasn't worried about him. She was worried about Mac facing a deadly adversary. "I'll saddle up Molly and follow you if you don't let me come."

After several long minutes, Mac finally gave a short nod, and Liv followed him out of the house and down the steps. It didn't take them long to reach an outer-lying building close to the dirt airstrip. Mac pulled two huge doors wide-open and disappeared inside. Liv took another deep breath and followed him.

The lights flicked on, and she was astounded at the sparkling white plane sitting in the middle of the spotless interior of the building. "I assume this is the small plane you were referring to?" She winced when she thought of the large melted hunk of metal sitting at the edge of the runway.

"It's a Cessna 172 single engine," he said as he moved around the plane doing what she assumed was a pre-flight check. Then he grabbed a bar attached to the wing and climbed into the pilot's seat. Liv rushed to the other side and grabbed the bar on her door. It was harder than it looked to get into the plane, but she was determined.

She had just gotten her seat belt on when a loud roar filled her ears as Mac started the engine. He motioned toward a headset after placing his own over his ears. She slipped it on and was startled when Mac's voice came through the headset. Shaking off the unsettling moment, she gripped the arms of her seat as the plane rolled forward, out of the building and onto the runway.

Liv had flown plenty of times, but always commercial. She'd never been in a small plane. Tempe had been a Blue Angel, but she never could have owned a plane like this one until recently.

The runway looked awfully short to her, and she spoke for the first time into the headset. "Are you sure we have enough space to take off?" Her voice came out sounding slightly high-pitched, but she couldn't help it. The plane was picking up speed, and they were quickly running out of runway. Pushing herself back into her seat—as if that would help anything—she closed her eyes as they came to the end but opened them when she felt the plane's wheels leave the ground.

Her heart skipped a beat at the big grin on Mac's face. It reminded Liv of how Tempe looked after she'd been flying.

"You love to fly, don't you?"

At her words, his grin slipped away and he became intently focused on his side window, searching the ground below. "I started flying choppers over the ranch when I was fifteen years old. I've been flying ever since."

Liv stared out her own window at the scrub brush, the foothills and the majestic Chisos Mountains in the distance. It was beautiful country, and she realized she'd missed it. She loved the conveniences of the city, but the breathtaking beauty of the Texas plains made something inside her shift, like a sense of coming home. If she still believed in God, she could almost think He was calling her back to Texas. She was shaken out of her musings when Mac's tightly controlled voice filled her headset.

"Bogeyman on the ground. We've got a SAM pointed straight at us."

Liv gripped the arms of her chair. "W-what's a SAM?"

"Surface-to-air missile" were his last words before the plane shot straight up into the air and started spinning faster than Liv could think. Just when she thought she'd lose her last meal, the aircraft leveled, and she swallowed back the acid sitting in her throat.

"Are we okay?" she managed to choke out seconds before Mac grimly shouted into her ear.

"Hang tight!"

Liv held on as tightly as she could and screamed when something slammed into the plane. It felt as if they'd been knocked out of the sky. Mac's voice in her ears was loud but fiercely controlled when he said, "Hang on, we're going down!"

FIFTEEN

Mac fought the controls of the plane and tried to keep enough altitude to get them away from the shooter. "Come on, baby," he mumbled. The control panel was lit up like a Christmas tree, and even as he smelled smoke, his hand was fisted around the yoke as he forced the plane back toward the house.

They lost more altitude, and he prayed through gritted teeth. "God, I need a little assistance here. Please help me land this plane."

"We're going to die and God's not going to save us," Liv yelled into his ear, even though she was sitting across from him. "We have to eject."

Calmness settled over him and he knew it was the good Lord at work. "This plane isn't equipped with an ejection feature," he said, giving her a quick glance. The horror written on her face had the opposite effect on him, settling his nerves even more.

Neither of them would die today. He'd prayed, and he'd been a Blue Angel. He knew every flying trick in the book. The plane lost even more altitude, and Mac started looking for a good place to set them down.

There was scrub brush, and up ahead he noted a good level spot, but it didn't matter. He had to get the plane on the ground.

"Hang on, I'm gonna land this thing." He was grateful the wheels dropped into landing position, and he braced himself when they bounced off the ground. He battled the controls to keep them as steady as possible, but every time one of the wheels hit a bush, the plane tilted to the side.

The muscles in his arms were clenched as he fought the rough landing. After the plane finally came to a shuddering halt, it took him a minute to unwrap his fingers from the controls. Closing his eyes, he thanked God for helping him, then glanced at Liv. Her eyes were squeezed shut, her porcelain skin was pasty white and she had a death grip on the armrests of her seat.

"Liv?" he said, but she didn't respond. He laid his tanned, callused fingers over her left hand and couldn't help but notice the contrast. Her fingers were long and elegant and soft, and his were work roughened. A rancher's hands. But at that moment their differences didn't seem to matter as much as they did before. They were alive.

He tried again. "Liv? Everything's okay. We landed."

Her eyes popped open, and she looked around, as if waking from a bad dream. "We made it?"

Mac grinned. He couldn't help himself. "Yes, ma'am."

Before he could take a solid breath, Liv fumbled with the seat belt and shot her upper body across the console between them, enveloping him in a big hug. Pulling back, she had the widest smile on her face he'd ever seen.

"We're alive!" she said before framing her hands on each side of his face and laying her soft lips against his. Even though he knew it couldn't go anywhere, he couldn't stop himself from kissing her back. As if finally realizing what she was doing, she pulled away and plopped back in her seat.

"I apologize. I didn't mean… Is that smoke I smell?" she asked, alarm ringing in her voice as she sat up straight.

Stunned by the sweetest and most moving kiss he'd ever experienced it took Mac a moment to answer. "Yes, yes, we should get out of here."

Fumbling with her door, she glared over her shoulder. "Why didn't you say so?"

Mac refrained from telling her she was the one kissing him and holding them up, because he was glad to see that spirited spark back in her eyes. He'd gotten them away from the shooter, but there might be more. Opening his own door, he hopped out of the plane, then circled the front to the other side and assisted a struggling Liv.

The smoke was getting heavier, so he pulled her along with him. They had to get as far away from the plane as possible. It was unlikely there would be an explosion, since that only really happened in movies, but smoke inhalation could be deadly. He came to a stop when he gauged there was enough distance between them and the plane, just to be on the safe side. They stood there, watching his aircraft smoke from the hit.

"Mac," she said haltingly, "I'm so sorry about your plane—about both of them."

He hated seeing the beautiful airplane burn, but the

insurance would help, and he had enough to cover what they didn't pay. "It's a material thing, and it can be replaced." He gazed into her soft brown eyes. "I'm just glad we're okay. How's your arm?" he asked gruffly, because what he really wanted to do was to lean down and kiss her.

She rubbed her bandaged arm. "It hurts, but I'll live."

"We might as well start walking back. That smoke could be a beacon for the men who shot us down if they are still out here."

"Don't you have a cell phone?"

"Yes, but reception isn't available this far out."

Liv gave a nervous glance around. "I see you have your larger gun. Do you still have your pistol?"

He patted the leg of his jeans. "Now that's something I never leave home without, living on a ranch and all," he drawled.

She held an open palm in front of him. "I'd like to borrow your pistol, please."

When he hesitated, she arched a brow. "I know how to shoot."

Why not, he thought. He'd seen her handle a gun when those two men tried to kidnap her on her side of the road and two people armed were better than one. Pulling it out, he handed it to her butt first. He smiled when she handled the weapon like an expert.

They'd made it about halfway to the house when Mac sensed movement behind them. Whipping around, he spotted the sun reflecting off the muzzle of a gun barely sticking out of a scrub brush and fired off a shot in that direction. The front of the gun disappeared, and he searched the area for more men but didn't see any.

Grabbing Liv, he hurried them forward at a faster pace. Hopefully, he'd hit the guy, but Mac prayed the shooter didn't have any buddies with him. He and Liv were out in the open, literally sitting ducks, ripe for the plucking.

Thankfully, Liv didn't ask questions, just moved as fast as she could. Mac stayed vigilant to their surroundings, and he breathed a sigh of relief when the house finally came into view. Things were spiraling out of control, and it was time to get tough.

Liv had stayed close to his side, and he was doubly astounded at her courage. The woman had grit. There were a lot of things he really admired about her, but the thick wall planted deeply between them was a simple matter of city versus country and her career aspirations that didn't include a husband and babies.

Except…had she ever actually said she didn't want a husband and babies, or had he only assumed that? And what's to say he couldn't live in the city part of the time? His job could be done anywhere. Shaken by his wandering thoughts, likely brought on by that sweet kiss, Mac was startled when Liv spoke.

"Mac, I apologize again for the destruction of your property. I know you didn't plan on this kind of situation when you offered to help me."

Her polite apology, as if they were total strangers, just rubbed him the wrong way. Especially after *she* had kissed *him*. "Well, now, you let me worry about that," he drawled, something he tended to do when he was aggravated or threatened in any way. His slower speech made him appear more relaxed, and people tended to underestimate him.

She pivoted, facing him dead-on with one of those elegant fingers pointed at him. "You always do that."

"What?" he asked, as if he didn't know what she was talking about.

"Your drawl and that 'well, then' and 'well, now.' I've noticed you always do that when you go on the defensive." She lifted her cute little chin, and Mac visualized all those brain cells rattling around in that head of hers, trying to get a bead on him. "A large part of my job as an attorney is to assess people and their mannerisms. It can help your case tremendously if you're able to read a witness properly."

"Yeah, well, I'm not a witness." He didn't want her trying to assess his personality.

She slowed as they stepped into the yard. "Mac, about that kiss. I didn't mean..."

Her words drifted away, and Mac got the message loud and clear. She didn't want him to take the kiss seriously. The thought made his gut burn. "I know. You have a ten-year career plan. Don't worry, I'm not going to ask you to marry me." His words came out harsher than he intended, but for some reason, her need to clarify her position didn't sit well with him. The fact that he didn't understand his own muddled feelings just made him testier.

Ten minutes later when they reached the house, Doc Hathaway's car had disappeared from the driveway, and Fort was casually leaning against a porch column. Not in any mood to deal with his brother, Mac took the steps two at a time. When he came alongside Fort, his nosy, irritating brother grinned after flipping his gaze between Liv and Mac. Anybody could sense the tension radiating off both of them.

"Man, I thought I had problems, but being around you makes me realize my life is a piece of cake."

Mac had had enough. "Your life *is* a piece of cake," he said, then couldn't stop himself from resorting to an old high school tactic. He rammed his shoulder into Fort's as he walked by, causing his brother to stumble back. He expected Fort to come at him, ready for a good tumble like the brothers always had in years past, but Fort only shook his head and laughed as Mac opened the front door and crossed the threshold.

"Bro, you've got it bad, and I for one am glad to see it."

Mac glanced over his shoulder and was gratified to see Liv give Fort an icy glare of disapproval as she followed Mac into the house. Spider was standing just outside the kitchen, stuffing one of Patsy's homemade cookies into his mouth. Mac grabbed his arm and headed down the hallway toward his basement office. "First, you're going to tell me your real name if you want to stay here, then we're going to work."

Liv watched Mac's broad back and Spider's skinny one as both men disappeared down the hall, and she got an itch between her shoulders like she sometimes did when a client or witness wasn't completely forthcoming. Mac was hiding something, but she couldn't imagine what it could be. She didn't want to think about throwing herself into his arms after their near crash and how good it had felt, so she took a relieved breath when Babette appeared on the stairs.

Just looking at her best friend decked out in the outlandish clothes she'd changed into caused Liv's spirits to lift as Babette rushed to her side with Boots tucked in her arms.

"Patsy told me you'd gone flying with Mac, trying to find those bad guys. Liv, that was dangerous."

Taking Babette by the arm, she guided her toward the living area and closed the door behind them. "You have no idea, but first, how is Cal doing?"

Babette drew in a deep breath and pressed Boots close to her heart. "Oh, Liv. The man saved my life. He took a bullet for me." Even after everything that had happened, Liv had to bite back a smile. Babette always leaned toward the dramatic.

"He saved both of us." Liv paused and searched for words that wouldn't hurt her friend's feelings but that would remove her from any danger. "Under the circumstances, I think you should go back to New York." When Babette opened her mouth to protest, Liv rushed on, "Mac was able to land the plane we were in, but someone shot at us and we almost crashed. We were shot at again while walking back."

Babette's chin dropped for a moment, but then she studied Liv with that shrewd look Liv had come to know very well. Babette's ultra-rich family was under the assumption there wasn't a brain under all that makeup, hair and colorful clothing, but Liv knew better. Her friend was both smart and savvy.

"Stop for a minute and look at yourself, Liv."

"What are you talking about?"

Babette reached out and touched the soft, worn fabric of her plaid shirt and stared pointedly at her jeans and well-worn cowboy boots. "As much as it pains me to say this, you belong here, sister of my heart," Babette said in her usual forthright manner.

Liv stiffened at her words. "I don't know what you mean. I love the city."

With a pitying look, Babette went to the heart of the matter. "Are you telling me you don't miss the wild Texas plains?" Before Liv had a chance to respond, Babette went on, "You're falling for Mac, aren't you?"

"No!" Liv answered, a little too forcefully. "It's only natural that I reminisce about growing up here, but my life is in the city. It's where I work." She took a deep breath. "You more than anyone know how hard I've worked to get where I am. My dream is to work for the Department of Justice, and I refuse to give that up."

"Would being a small-town attorney be so bad?" Babette shifted her eyes away. "You know my parents tried to mold me into something that would have destroyed me. They didn't think I had the brains to run the family business, so they tried to marry me off to someone they deemed appropriate." She looked straight at Liv. "You know the story. I went out and made it on my own terms by opening my dog-grooming stores. Plans change all the time. Don't place yourself in a box. Let nature take its course and see what happens."

Liv wrapped her arms around Babette and Boots and hugged them fiercely. "What would I do without you?" she whispered.

Babette pulled back and grinned. "That's why I'm staying here until this mess is resolved. You need me. I have excellent managers at the stores, and I haven't taken a vacation in forever."

Liv moved away and swiped at a tear threatening to fall past her lashes. "So much has happened in such a short amount of time, and didn't you go to the Bahamas just last month?"

Babette gave a loud, boisterous laugh that never failed to make Liv feel better. "Well, it seems like forever." Then she got that stubborn look on her face that Liv also knew too well. "I'm planting my feet here in Texas until you're safe and Cal is back on his feet."

"Babette, about Cal—"

Her friend cut her off by waving her entire arm in the air. "He's already explained about being homeless. People end up on the streets for many reasons. That doesn't mean he's not a nice person. The guy not only saved my life, he's extremely knowledgeable about dogs. Unexpected things can happen to anyone."

"Are you, uh—"

Babette shot her a disgruntled look. "I'm not interested in him that way. After my last fiasco, I'm taking a break from the dating scene."

Babette kissed the top of Boots' head and gave it one last shot. "There sure is a lot of energy sparking around you and Mac. You sure you won't give it a chance?"

"Babette," Liv growled, drawing her name out.

"Fine. I won't bring it up again."

"Good. Did Patsy settle you into a room?"

"Oh, Liv," Babette breathed, "it's absolutely lovely. The Texas motif is astounding. I've never stayed in a room like that."

Fort came sauntering through the front door, the evening sun creating a picture-perfect backdrop for his tanned complexion and dark hair. The man could be a movie star.

He and Babette started bantering, and Liv decided it was a good time to slip away. She wanted to see what Mac and Spider—and what a name!—were doing in Mac's basement computer room.

Just as she turned, her cell phone rang, causing her to tense, afraid it might be Mr. Kale. She gritted her teeth and took several steps away from Babette and Fort before glancing at the number. A chill shot up her spine when she stared at the words *Unknown Caller* written across her screen. She moved farther away and took the call, slowly placing the phone close to her ear.

"Yes?"

"Hello, Olivia." Mr. Kale's smug tone, as if he held all the cards, caused goose bumps to pop up on her arms. "I believe I've proven I can get to you and your friends at any time." His voice hardened. "One of Mac Dolan's friends has been snooping in places best left alone. We almost caught up with him—" he gave a false sigh "—but it's just as well he came running to the ranch. It makes it so much easier to erase everyone at one time."

Perspiration made the phone in Liv's hand slippery, but years spent in front of a jury kept her voice firm. "You set me up to take the fall for a murder I didn't commit. You're evil."

His soft chuckle set her teeth on edge. "Think whatever you will, but here are your choices. You can stay tucked away at Mac Dolan's ranch and all of you will die, or you can slip out tonight and meet one of my men at the highway and I won't touch any of your friends."

Now that she was over the initial shock, Liv started forming a plan. She wouldn't allow anything to happen to all the people at the ranch, or at her family's ranch, for that matter, but neither was she going to go down without a fight, because it was clear Mr. Kale and whoever his associates were wanted her dead.

"And how do I know you won't kill all of them anyway, even if I do as you say?"

"Ah, Miss Calloway, think for a moment. You're a firsthand witness. All your friends know is what you've chosen to share with them. They have no evidence against me or my firm, and I plan to keep it that way. Removing all of you would present a bigger challenge, but I can manage it, if need be."

Not really having a choice, Liv said, "Fine, I'll leave the house after midnight," and hoped Mr. Kale wouldn't hurt anyone she cared about.

The phone clicked in her ear, and he was gone. Her shoulder throbbed, and she stood there, gripping the device in her hand.

"Liv." Babette's voice sounded like it was coming from far away. "Liv! Is everything okay?"

Liv looked up and forced her lips into a smile. "It's fine. Nothing to worry about. I'm going to my room for a while to rest."

Babette nodded, concern written on her face as Liv walked away. She had very little time to make plans, and her life depended on them.

SIXTEEN

Mac tapped the keyboard of his powerful computer system, with Spider next to him at an adjoining console. Glancing sideways, Mac marveled at the blur of Spider's fingers on the keyboard.

"Dude, you got some serious RAM and CPUs going on this thing." Spider cut him a sly glance. "'Course, you are with the FBI."

Mac stopped typing and swiveled his chair to face the malnourished guy sitting across from him. "What's your name?"

Spider shrugged razor-thin shoulders and glanced away. "I don't give out my real name. It's a kind of protection, you know?"

Mac had had enough. His gut told him time was running out and they still had zero proof against Liv's boss. "Tell me your name or you can get back inside that ratty car of yours and take your chances elsewhere. Name!" he repeated forcefully.

"Aw. Fine! It's Theodore Rivera," he said painfully, "but please, call me Spider."

"Okay, Spider, what makes you think I'm connected

with the FBI?" Mac wasn't happy with his online associate.

"Okay," Spider snapped, "so I did a little snooping around and found out you contract out with the FBI, so sue me. That's why I headed this way when those guys came after me. It's really your fault that I'm here."

Mac wanted to strangle the kid, but that wouldn't help matters. He needed information fast, and Spider was good at what he did. Spider's eyes widened as Mac brought him up to speed concerning Liv.

"Wow! I must've raised some red flags when I went hunting," Spider exclaimed.

Mac agreed but only said, "Let's get to work."

Quiet settled in the room, interrupted only by the clack of keys on the keyboards until Patsy knocked on the basement door and yelled, "Dinner's on the table."

Mac didn't even look up, but Spider stopped typing. "What?" Mac ground out.

"I'm hungry, man. I drove down from Jersey and haven't eaten since yesterday except for a cookie."

Mac stopped working. He wanted to check on Liv anyway and make sure their rough landing hadn't damaged her shoulder any further. "Fine. Let's go."

Spider scrambled out of the seat like a starving teenager, and Mac followed him up the stairs. As soon as they hit the hallway, Spider followed the smell of fried chicken all the way to the kitchen, where the Dolans took most of their meals, unless the whole family was there. When Spider came to a sudden stop, Mac bumped into him.

"Dude, this is like a picture in a cooking magazine."

Mac looked around his shoulder and saw the table

was laden with good, home-cooked food. Fried chicken, a heaping bowl of mashed potatoes with gravy on the side. Green beans and homemade yeast rolls. A pie cooled on the counter, ready for dessert that Mac knew would be served with ice cream. He could practically hear the kid drooling. He poked Spider in the back. "Take a seat."

Everyone was there except for Cal, whom Patsy had probably already taken a plate to. Mac sat down across from Liv. Her color was off, and she appeared to be distracted. He nodded at Patsy, and they bowed their heads. He heard the clatter of silverware and figured it was Spider. Once Mac said a short prayer of thanks, he opened his eyes, and Patsy started passing around platters of food. He was glad to see Liv put a nice portion of mashed potatoes on her plate. Spider finally stopped heaping green beans on his plate when everyone turned to stare at him.

"What?"

"There's no way you can eat all that food," Mac challenged.

Spider grinned and scooped up another helping. "I haven't had food like this, like, in my whole life. This is real chicken, not those weird things the fast-food joints call chicken, you know?" Spider added when the large platter was placed in his hands. He took a breast and two wings.

"Liv," Mac said as he took a piece of chicken for himself, "how's your shoulder and arm doing?"

Her smile was forced. "I'm fine."

Babette groaned when she took a bite of crispy meat.

"This meal will put five pounds on me that I'll have to lose, but I don't care."

Fort piped in. "You look fabulous, Babette. You don't need to worry about a few pounds."

Mac inwardly rolled his eyes, and Babette preened. "Why, thank you, Fort. It's not true, but I appreciate the sentiment."

The conversation rolled around the table, but Mac kept studying Liv. Something was off with her, but he couldn't quite put his finger on it. Babette supplied part of the answer.

"That phone call you received earlier really upset you, didn't it, Liv?"

Liv's smile was strained. "No. It was nothing important."

Mac went for casual, but he really wanted to grill her. "What was it about? Who called?"

She shrugged and pushed the food she hadn't eaten around on her plate. "Nothing, really. Just someone from work who didn't know I'd left the city."

He swallowed a bite of perfectly cooked meat. "The security team Dean recommended will be here in the morning."

Fort took a big sip of tea. "How's the youngest Dolan boy faring?"

It was asked very casually, but everyone in the family worried about Dean and his current career in the Navy SEALs. "He sounded fine."

Mac could practically hear Spider inhaling his food beside him, but he concentrated on Liv. He wanted to know more about the phone call she had received, but he couldn't ask with everyone around.

Patsy changed the subject. "How's things on the new house coming along, Mac?"

That got Babette's attention. "You're building a new house?"

Mac didn't want to discuss house plans, he wanted answers from Liv, but he had to get through this meal first. "Yep. Mom and Dad were gracious enough to sell me a portion of the ranch."

He didn't quite understand the gleam in Liv's friend's eye.

"Sounds like you plan to stay in Texas."

"Yes," he said, even though the idea that had popped into his head earlier still lingered, and he added, "for the most part."

Conversation swirled around him for the rest of the meal, and he was glad when Patsy served dessert. He was afraid Spider might burst by the time he was done, but finally, *finally*, everyone finished and Patsy cleared the table. Babette and Liv offered to help with the dishes, but Patsy shooed everyone out, claiming they'd only be in the way. When everyone drifted to the living room, Mac gently took Liv by the arm and pulled her down the hall in the other direction, where they'd have a modicum of privacy.

"What was the phone call about? Did you get another call from Mr. Kale?" he asked. The thought of that snake threatening her set his gut on fire.

He didn't miss the slight tremble of her lips before she pasted on a wide, fake smile. "No, no, it really was just a coworker thinking I was still in the city. One of the junior associates was working overtime, closing out a case, and they had a few questions. Nothing to worry about. Mac, I can't tell you how much I appreciate everything you've done." She paused. "I'm pretty tired after everything that's happened. I'm heading to bed early."

She slipped away, and Mac followed her to the foot of the stairs, watching her until she disappeared. He was sure of one thing—Liv Calloway was up to something, and he was determined to find out what. He had the oddest feeling that she was saying goodbye, and he wouldn't allow her to walk out of here and get herself killed.

Liv leaned against the door inside of her bedroom and closed her eyes. She hadn't wanted to deceive Mac, but it was the only way to keep him alive. He was in the military and had flown some of the finest planes the Blue Angels had to offer, but in reality, he was just a cowboy, albeit one who made a good bit of money as a financial planner. She considered the security arriving tomorrow, but they couldn't all hide here forever, and so far, they hadn't been able to find proof against Mr. Kale and his horrible associates. If she didn't do as her boss demanded and meet one of his goons tonight, people might die. She couldn't live with that.

This was what all the hard work she'd spent her whole adult life on had come down to. There was a good chance she'd be dead before ever having the chance to fully live. She wished she still believed in God. If that were the case, she'd be on her knees right now, but she couldn't quite bring herself to do it.

She thought of Mac and his dark brown eyes that seemed to penetrate to the very core of her being.

Shaking off her maudlin thoughts, she straightened her shoulders. Her granddaddy Dill Calloway would tell her to *git* some grit and fight, and that's exactly what she planned to do. She wouldn't give up, because she had a lot to live for. Mac's strong, solid face swam across her mind at that last thought, but she ignored it and started planning.

A glance at the clock on the bedside stand showed she had three hours until midnight to prepare. She thought longingly of Mac's pistol tucked snugly inside his ankle holster, but a gun would be risky anyway. She might get shot in the process of trying to defend herself. It was probably best to stay away from that particular weapon. Words had always been her weapon of choice, and she would use them, but she needed a backup.

Tamping down the panic trying to claw its way to the surface, she took a deep breath and methodically searched the room. Her gaze landed on the bedside stand, where there were three possibilities—an ink pen, a set of keys belonging to her burned rental car and a coffee mug.

She sat on the side of the bed and slumped her shoulders, staring at the three pitiful items. If she got close enough—she shivered at the thought—she could stab them in the eye with the pen or keys. The mug would be awkward to conceal, but if she could hit them in the head hard enough, that might stop them long enough for her to escape.

And what would happen if she did escape? Mr. Kale would destroy everyone she loved. Her best option, if they didn't kill her on the spot, was to go with them and try to find proof against Kale, then escape as quickly as possible.

She would have to work fast, because Mr. Kale had already tracked down Spider, and he was the one most likely to be able to track the email placed in her Sent box.

She fell back on the bed and stared at the ceiling, analyzing her plan. Words were her life. How could she use that? Hopefully she could convince Mr. Kale that she'd had a change of heart and wanted to join forces with him. That would definitely give her more time. The more she thought about it, the better the plan sounded. Mr. Kale was greedy and power-hungry. She could use that.

It would be hard to play the part, but she could do it. She'd swayed many jurors with her gift of gab. The first person she'd have to convince would be the man Kale sent to pick her up tonight. It would be the ultimate mediation, a negotiation for her life.

A knock sounded on her door, and it opened just as she sat back up on the bed. Liv's smile was genuine when Babette walked in carrying Misty and Boots. As Babette leaned down, Misty wiggled out of her arms and scooted over to Liv, her tiny claws clicking on the hardwood floor. She scooped her precious baby up and showered her with kisses. Tears sprang to her eyes when she thought of never seeing her dog again.

"Babette," she managed to get out, "if anything happens to me, I want your promise that you'll take care of Misty."

Babette sat down beside her, placed Boots on the bed and wrapped both arms around Liv. "Nothing is going to happen to you. You're safe here, and Mac said more security is coming tomorrow. No matter what happens, you know I'll always take care of Misty." She pulled back. "Now, I know you've been under a lot of pressure, but everything's under control."

Liv wanted to scream and yell at the injustice of everything that was happening to her, but she restrained herself and changed the subject. "How's Cal doing? His injury seemed to be worse than mine."

Babette slapped a hand across her heart. "I still can't believe that man risked his life to save mine. He's doing much better. Patsy sent him up some of the best-smelling vegetable soup ever to hit my nose. I made sure he ate every bite before I came down for dinner. It just amazes me that a stranger, in this day and age, would risk their life like that."

They sat in silence for a moment, which was unusual for both of them, then Babette, with her usual forthright fashion, asked a personal question. "Not that I want my best friend in the whole world to leave New York, but aren't you just the tiniest bit interested in Mac Dolan? It was obvious at dinner, with him sneaking looks at you the whole time we were eating, that he's interested in you."

Liv sighed. "It doesn't matter whether either one of us is interested or not. It would never work, Babette. He has both feet planted in Texas, and I'm returning to the city as soon as this is over."

"And whom do you plan to work for? Because when this is over, I'm hoping your boss will be put away for a long, long time."

When Liv didn't say anything, Babette hugged her

again and stood. "I don't want to add to your worries. It's just something to think about. I'll let you get some rest."

She headed for the door, and Misty followed Babette and Boots. It was a perfect situation for her dog when Liv sneaked out later. "Let Misty sleep with Boots. You know they'll love that."

Babette stopped and scooped Misty into her spare arm. She smiled. "Don't worry. Things will look brighter in the morning when that extra security gets here," she said and left the room.

Liv got up and closed the door behind them, then lay back in bed, her mind racing. If she couldn't convince Mr. Kale or his goons that she was willing to collude with them, she might very well have to fight for her life. His goon could try to kill her on the spot. If that was the case, she'd have to come up with another plan to protect those she loved.

Glancing at the clock on the wall, she watched the minutes tick by. She thought of her granddaddy, of Tempe and her new husband, Ewen. Of Riley, her voracious niece, and actually smiled when she pictured Aunt Effie and Dudley. Her aunt and Ewen's friend were complete opposites, but it seemed to work.

She listened as the house and its occupants settled, and at eleven thirty, using the same focus she used in the courtroom, she methodically rose from the bed and set about getting ready to slip out of the house.

She kept her emotions contained. If she thought much about what she was getting ready to do, she wouldn't be able to go through with it. Useless though it might be, she carried the pen, keys and mug with her. Fifteen minutes before midnight, she cracked her door open, stepped into the hallway and headed down the stairs.

Opening the front door, she slipped through and faced the darkness of the night, in more ways than one.

SEVENTEEN

Mac's stomach clenched and he gritted his teeth as he stepped from a hidden nook behind the stairwell and watched Liv furtively slip out the front door. He hadn't known until this moment how much he wanted her to be innocent—and his gut was screaming that she was—but this scenario didn't bode well for that feeling.

He'd wait a moment or so before following her. Just as he took a step forward, he heard his basement door open and close down the hall, and footsteps headed toward him. Spider rushed forward waving a wad of papers in his hand.

"I thought you were in bed."

"Dude, I'm a night owl. I found what you wanted. It's all right here."

Spider was talking so fast, Mac held up a hand. "I'm in a hurry here. What are you jabbering about?"

"The email. I can't track it back to the original server yet, but I can prove Liv Calloway didn't send it from her computer."

Mac's pulse beat rapidly in his neck, and his heart soared. Liv was innocent! But as soon as that thought crossed his mind, he questioned why she would sneak out of the house at midnight, and the answer threw a bucket of cold water on his short-lived celebration.

If she was innocent, there was only one reason Liv would try to leave the ranch: to prevent anyone she cared about from getting hurt. The call she had received earlier must have been from Mr. Kale, spouting all kinds of threats.

He had to get a move on. "Spider, good work. I'll talk to you later."

He slipped through the front door and moved silently into the night, then stopped to listen. He didn't need Barnie to track her. His hunting skills were phenomenal.

Yes, there—several squirrels and other wildlife stirring as something passed them.

She was headed toward the highway. Mac moved quietly and efficiently. Military training and hunting had taught him how to meld into whatever terrain he found himself in. The animals didn't stir as he passed. He locked down all emotion and prayed that God would lead the way, as he did every time he found himself in any kind of dangerous situation.

An owl hooted off to his side, and he felt a slight breeze against his cheeks. There were trees mixed in with the scrub brush, offering plenty of places for cover. He heard low, murmured voices before he saw anyone, so he moved closer. What he observed had his pulse racing again, this time in fear. Both Tommy and Gordon Genovese, Mr. Kale's hired goons, stood before Liv. One of them had a gun pointed at her heart.

From a vast amount of practice, Mac willed his heart rate to slow and waited to strike.

"You think just because you're a hotshot fancy lawyer, you're smarter than we are, don't you?" one of the goons said, his words laced with malice.

Liv had a temper on her, and Mac prayed she'd stay calm, but he should have known better. She was a professional, after all.

"Gentlemen, after everything we've been through together, I'm sure we can come to some sort of understanding."

One of the guys—Mac didn't know which one was which—spat on the ground and snarled, "Your time has run out, lady, and we don't have to do anything you say."

She released a dramatic sigh, then said, "If your boss instructed you to get rid of me, that would be terribly unfortunate."

One of the men, the one without a gun in his hand, took the bait. "How come?"

"Shut up, Gordon."

So, Tommy Genovese was the one holding the gun, Mac thought.

"Don't tell me to shut up."

Tommy glared at his brother and turned his attention back to Liv, raising his weapon.

Mac had his pistol in his hand and got ready to move, but he eased his finger off the trigger when she chuckled. He didn't doubt she fooled the Genovese men, but Mac heard the underlying strain behind her laugh, and it tightened his gut.

"If you shoot me here, do you realize how much evidence you'll leave behind? It won't take a good cop but a few days to connect you to the crime and arrest you."

"Tommy," Gordon whined, "I ain't going back to the slammer. I'd rather die first."

"Shut up, Gordon. No one is going to jail."

Liv chimed back in. "If you boys would listen to me, no one will go to jail." Both men looked back at Liv, and Mac had to admire her poise in such a dangerous situation. He was coming to admire a lot about the spitfire standing off against two large men. He wondered what her plan was, because he didn't doubt now that she had one.

"What I've been trying to tell you is that I'm ready to join forces with Mr. Kale. I'll be a huge asset to him, and he won't be happy if you kill me before I get a chance to talk to him."

Tommy stood there, apparently mulling over her words. She was the first to bring up Kale, and Mac wondered if the Genovese boys even realized she'd said their boss's name—the man who'd sent them to kill her. Maybe she was recording the conversation. Mac was trying to figure out Liv's game plan when he caught the movement of a shadow in the scrub brush directly behind the two brothers. Did they bring backup? Or had Mr. Kale sent someone to make sure the two men did the job properly?

He'd been in plenty of dicey situations, but this was different, because he didn't know how many players he was up against, and Liv… Nothing could happen to her. He wouldn't allow it.

Things had just gone from bad to worse in a matter of seconds. He methodically went through every possible scenario in his head while critically watching the movement of all the players.

Liv threw her hands wide. "What have you got to lose? At least this way you won't be wanted for murder. You can dispose of me later if Mr. Kale doesn't like what I have to say."

Mac was glad Spider had told him of her innocence, because she sounded convincing, as if she would really join forces with that scum of the earth.

"C'mon, Tommy," Gordon whined again, "let's take her to Mr. Kale and see what he says."

"We're supposed to get rid of her, you fool. The boss won't be happy if we bring her in, and we won't get paid."

They had just confirmed who their boss was, and Mac was a witness. The moonlight revealed Liv's clenched hands, and Mac wanted to swoop in and get rid of the threat, but he couldn't make a move with that gun pointed straight at her.

Mac prayed she wouldn't get hurt and forced himself to be patient. His chest expanded in an odd sort of pride when Liv tried a new tactic.

"You do realize that Mr. Kale will have to get rid of both of you after you kill me, right? He would never leave anyone alive who could come back and cause him problems. Your best option is to take me to him. If after that he wants you to get rid of me, you'll have more options in the city. I'm sure you've heard about the Texas Rangers. They're tough people and won't stop until they track you down."

Mac wanted to strangle Liv and kiss her at the same time. How could she speak so casually about her own demise when she had to be scared out of her mind? The shadow behind the Genovese men shifted slightly, and

Mac went on high alert. His body was relaxed, but he was ready to spring into action at a moment's notice.

Gordon whimpered, but Tommy raised the gun higher. "We were hired to do a job, and we're gonna do it."

Time had run out. Mac's body tensed as he readied himself to spring forward, but before he could move, a host of shadows melted out of the woods carrying some serious firepower and surrounded Liv and the Genovese men.

As armed men appeared out of the darkness and surrounded them, Liv felt a lightness in her head, a sure sign of fainting, and it was all she could do to hold herself together. Were they sent by Mr. Kale to make sure the job got done? If so, it was definitely overkill. The whole scene was surreal, like she was starring in a horror movie. She realized she hadn't breathed and forced herself to part her lips and let the air flow in and out.

Her hope soared when a guy with paint smeared on his face guttered out a command. "You have one second to drop the weapon."

Two of the men on her left suddenly whipped away from her and pointed their guns toward the darkness. Liv almost had a heart attack when Mac stepped out from behind a bush with both hands up before he slowly laid his pistol on the ground. She rushed toward him and one of the men grabbed her by the arm, but she jerked away and ran to Mac.

She was so glad to see him, she threw herself against his chest without even thinking. Two strong arms wrapped around her waist, and he felt so warm and safe, but she finally released him only to find him scowling down at her.

She heard a scuffle behind her and whipped around to see Tommy had relinquished his gun and the men had tied both of the goons' hands behind their backs. The reality of that hit her solid. Mr. Kale would come after her friends and family, unless they stopped him first—which she was determined to do.

She turned to find Mac talking to one to the men who had rescued her, and she interrupted their conversation, facing off with Mac. "You just ruined everything."

The small lines between Mac's eyes snapped together, and she noticed a tic in his jaw. "Well, now, Miss Calloway—" his slow speech indicated irritation, she'd discovered "—it seems to me you were about to get yourself killed." He motioned toward the man standing next to him, who was dressed in dark clothing with something smeared on his face. "These are friends of my brother Dean. The security team I hired. They came in earlier than expected. You might want to thank them for saving your life."

The man made her feel like a heel and Liv fumed inside, but she smiled at the man standing there acting very interested in the dynamics playing out between her and Mac. "I certainly appreciate everything you did tonight."

A set of white teeth shone in the darkness. "You're welcome, ma'am." He nodded at Mac. "The place is clear. Do you want to call the police or question those two guys first?"

The police? "Mac, we definitely need to talk to them

first. We don't need to call the police." Liv's words flew out of her mouth.

For the first time, Mac grinned, as if he knew something she didn't, then gave instructions. "Put them in the tack room in the barn. We might be able to make a deal that will benefit both us and them."

The guy gave a sharp nod. "Done. You won't see us, but we'll be around." Liv was amazed when he just faded into the darkness.

"How do they do that?" she wondered out loud. "And what do you mean, we might make a deal with those two goons? They were on the verge of killing me."

Mac took her by the elbow. "We can talk while we head to the house."

Liv went with him, but she stumbled when her knees almost buckled beneath her. Mac held on to her elbow and pulled her toward him, bringing their faces into close proximity. Her heart raced when he lowered his head and soft lips touched hers. Her knees went weak again before he finished the sweetest kiss she'd ever had and lifted his head. Staring into her eyes, he ruined the precious moment.

"Did you have a death wish, coming out here alone?"

That just burned, especially since she was still reeling from that kiss. "I'll have you know I had everything under control." That wasn't true, but she wasn't ready to concede that to Mac.

"Uh-huh."

She stomped toward the house, but with his long strides, he didn't have any trouble keeping up with her. She slowed down after a short distance, because she was still shaky. "Okay," she mumbled, "maybe things had gotten out of hand, but Mr. Kale threatened my family and friends, and I had to do something. I had a good plan."

"Uh-huh, and what was your big plan?"

She stumbled again, and the coffee mug fell out of her jacket pocket. Mac stopped and picked it up. He stared at it long and hard before lifting his head. His jaw was ticking again.

"And what did you plan on using this for?"

Liv grabbed the mug out of his hand and stalked forward again. "You could injure someone gravely with this heavy porcelain mug."

He caught up with her, and she stopped when he placed a hand on her elbow. "Talk to me, Liv."

All the fire in her belly was doused at his soft statement, and her shoulders slumped. "I didn't know what to do. So many dangerous things have happened, and Mr. Kale made terrible threats if I refused to give myself up." She lifted her chin and stared him in the eye. "You have to understand, I couldn't let anyone else get hurt."

"You have a big heart, and I understand your reasoning, but, Liv, you could have been killed."

It dawned on her what she'd said to Gordon and Tommy, and she grabbed Mac by the arm. He would think she was guilty, and she had to convince him otherwise. "What I said to Mr. Kale's men—I only said it so I could get close enough to find proof against my boss for what he did. I didn't really mean it when I said I wanted to join forces with him."

She was talking too fast, but she couldn't stand the thought of Mac thinking she would do something so horrible. He placed a finger on her lips, effectively stopping her words, and grinned.

"I'm spilling my guts here and you're grinning," she said against his fingers.

"I'm smiling because right before I followed you out here, Spider told me he found proof that you didn't send those emails. He hasn't been able to trace them back to the original server, but he's working on it."

Relief hit Liv so hard she swayed, and Mac wrapped his arms around her and whispered in her ear, "Everything's gonna be okay."

She was relieved because she could prove her innocence, but everything wasn't going to be okay. It was hard to pull out of her protective cocoon, but Liv forced herself to move away. "If I'm not dead, Mr. Kale will go after everyone I care for. It's not over. I can't hide here forever, and he can get to Tempe and Riley and anyone at the Calloway ranch at any time. I know Ewen likely has an invisible fortress surrounding my family, but no one will be safe until Mr. Kale is stopped."

"Well, now—" Mac smiled slowly "—I reckon I have an idea or two about that."

EIGHTEEN

Mac's arms fell to his side when Liv pulled away, leaving him feeling empty, an emotion he wasn't quite comfortable with, so he focused on the problem at hand.

"What kind of plan?" she asked, and he heard the hope filling her voice. "How can you stop Mr. Kale from coming after me and the people I care about?"

Mac wondered if he was included in the people Liv cared about, but he would never ask. The barn came into view, and he started walking in that direction. "First we're going to have a nice little chat with our two guests."

Liv effectively stopped him by touching his arm. "I won't allow you to do anything that might get you into trouble. As a matter of fact, now that Spider can prove my innocence, maybe we should call the police."

"And how will that protect your family, Liv? If Mr. Kale becomes desperate, he might up the ante if he gets wind of what's going on. I'd rather handle this myself." Two small lines creased her brows, marring that perfect face, and he wanted to smooth them away.

"Okay. What are you going to say to the two men?"

"C'mon and you'll find out."

She followed him to the barn, where the lights had been left on by Dean's friends. Mac stomped down the center aisle, fury filling him as he got closer to the men who'd tried to harm Liv. They had been placed in the tack room.

Liv bumped into him when he stopped at the entrance. Both men were sitting in a corner, their backs propped against the side of the room with their hands tied behind them. Tommy managed a halfway decent sneer when Mac moved closer and squatted in front of them.

"Well, now," Mac drawled and heard a slight chuckle behind him. At least Liv had relaxed enough to make a sound that was music to his ears. He stared hard at the two men glaring back at him. "We can do this the easy way or the hard way. That'll be up to you."

Tommy studied him a moment, then with a touch of bewilderment lacing his words, asked, "Who *are* you?"

Mac knew what he was asking. Tommy's street survival instincts allowed him to recognize something in Mac that most civilians never noticed: he'd do whatever it took to get the job done. Mac gave him a slow smile. "That depends. We can help each other, and I'll put in a good word for you when you go to trial for attempted murder. Or I can call the police now. I'm sure your boss would be happy to bail you out, but I don't reckon you'll live very long after that."

Gordon grunted, but Mac kept his eyes trained on Tommy. He appeared to be the leader of the two.

Tommy shrugged and looked away. "He'll kill us anyway, so why should I help you?"

Mac got to the heart of the matter. "Because we're gonna take Mr. Kale down."

A jerky laugh came out of Tommy's mouth. "Right."

Mac spoke softly and with deadly precision. "You think I can't take your boss down?"

Tommy stared at Mac long and hard. "What do you want me to do?"

"How did you plan to contact your boss after the deed was done?"

"I was supposed to text him. Phones don't work too good out here, but texts go through most of the time."

"Do we have a deal?" Mac asked. Tommy dipped his chin, and Mac took that as a yes.

"Where's your phone?"

"Somewhere outside the door there. Your friends—" he gave Mac a dark look "—took everything out of my pockets and put it out there."

"Liv," Mac said without taking his eyes off Tommy, "see if you can find the phone."

He heard Liv moving around. "I found it!" she exclaimed and passed it to him over his shoulder.

Mac stood and held the phone in front of him. "What's your password and where do you have him listed?" Tommy told him the security code, and then Mac located the number. "What would you have sent?"

"Two words. *It's done.*"

Mac could literally feel the anger rolling off Liv behind him when Tommy calmly, with no emotion whatsoever, said the words that would have confirmed her death. She'd been through a lot tonight, and he needed to get this wrapped up. He wouldn't put it past her to kick one of these guys just to vent her fear and frustration.

He sent the text and waited to see if there would be a response. It wasn't long coming. Good. Get back to New York. I have a job waiting for you.

Mac wondered what that job would be, and it made him even more determined to stop this scourge on society. "I know the local sheriff. The county jail is in Alpine, and you'll be picked up in the morning. I'll ask him to hold you there until we get things under control. Your boss won't know where you are."

That would give Mac time to come up with a plan to take Liv's boss down. And take him down he would. The image of Tommy holding a gun on Liv would stay with him the rest of his life.

He turned to leave and caught Liv by the shoulders as she tried to slip past him. The fire blazing in her eyes brought a grin to his face. "Now, darlin', you don't wanna go and do something you'll regret later. You are a representative of the law."

"That man was going to kill me," she said through gritted teeth.

"I know, but we have what we need." He pulled her along the aisle until they were outside. She stomped out of the barn, and he much preferred her anger versus the fear she'd tried so hard to hide.

"C'mon. We should get some sleep."

Liv stopped before they climbed the front porch steps. "Mac, I can never thank you enough for everything you've done. You were willing to risk your life for me out there." Her long dirty-blond hair hung in disarray around her shoulders, and those big, grateful brown eyes staring at him were filled with gratitude.

Mac didn't want her gratitude. He wanted… He

didn't know what he wanted. "We should get some sleep. I have an idea, but we'll regroup tomorrow morning," he replied, more briskly than he'd intended.

He thought a flicker of hurt crossed her eyes, but he must have been mistaken, because she turned on her heel and climbed the steps, disappearing into the house. Slowly, Mac went up the steps and through the front door.

In the foyer, Spider appeared from the kitchen with a half-eaten cookie in his hand. He took one look at Mac and spoke around a mouthful of food. "Hey, man, what's got you looking like your dog died? Liv came in before you did, and man, she was one unhappy-looking lady." Spider grinned, and Mac noticed chocolate chip pieces stuck to his teeth. "Hey, if you're having woman trouble, I'm, like, here if you need to talk."

Barnie came ambling out of the kitchen behind Spider, and Mac rubbed his dog's head while staring at the skinny guy standing in front of him.

"Don't you ever sleep?"

Spider waved the cookie in the air. "I'm a—"

"Night owl. That's good, because we have a lot of work to do tonight. We'll be leaving first thing tomorrow morning, heading to the Big Apple."

Liv tossed and turned all night and woke the next morning with a slight headache. As she lay in bed replaying everything that had happened the previous night, she shivered, thinking how close she'd come to dying. If the security hadn't shown up, Mac could have been killed, too, and that wasn't acceptable.

It was time to go on the defense and beat Mr. Kale

at his own game. Her boss now thought she was dead, and that could play to her advantage. Strategy was an intricate part of being an attorney, and it was high time she used it. A workable plan was just forming in her mind when her bedroom door flew open and two dogs, followed by Babette, came trotting into the room with joyous barks of greeting.

Liv leaned over the side of the bed and picked up Misty off the floor, giving her smooches while the dog licked her all over the face. Babette chuckled, and Liv glanced at her friend, not surprised to find Babette and Boots wearing matching outfits. Today it was a fitted powder-blue pants outfit trimmed with lavender lace. Boots was wearing the same colors in a cute doggie vest. Babette always combined unusual colors, and they seemed to work for her. She should have been born in the South. New Yorkers wore black, for the most part.

"Rise and shine," her best friend said. "Mac announced that we're leaving for New York within the hour."

That got Liv's attention. "What?"

Babette moved farther into the room. "That man of yours—"

"He's not my man," Liv responded forcefully.

"—told Spider to get ready to leave, and I informed Mac that we're going with the two of you. Cal is well enough to travel, and he'll be going with us, too."

Cal was going with them? Liv's head was reeling, but she'd ask Babette about that later. Mac had said they would regroup this morning. He hadn't said a word about going to New York. Liv scrambled out of bed, and Babette followed her to the bathroom.

"Heart sister of mine, you desperately need a manicure and a hair salon."

The matter-of-fact statement almost made Liv laugh, at least until she saw her reflection in the mirror. Her hair was sticking out everywhere, but she only took time to run a brush through the tangles and splash water on her face and brush her teeth.

She had to find out what was happening. Liv dressed quickly, and Babette followed her down the stairs to the kitchen, where everyone was gathered.

Mac swallowed a mouthful of breakfast before speaking. "Grab something to eat and pack your bags. We're leaving soon."

Liv had a million questions, but she stifled them because she realized that going back to the city fit perfectly into the plans solidifying in her mind. She grabbed a cup of coffee and two pieces of toast and headed upstairs to pack.

Forty-five minutes later, after saying goodbye to everyone staying at the ranch, Liv stood on the side of the runway with Misty in her arms, completely flabbergasted. The man must have some major contacts to make this happen, which brought forth more questions she didn't have time to ask. "Where in the world did you get another plane?"

"I borrowed it and had someone deliver it last night," Mac answered irritably. Liv almost laughed, watching him prod their small group onto the aircraft. Babette was clutching Boots to her chest while giving Cal a helping hand up the steps. Barnie ambled up behind Spider, and Mac motioned Liv forward.

He followed her up, closed the door behind them and

disappeared into the cockpit. Liv sat down in one of the plush seats across from Cal. A table separated the four leather chairs. Another grouping was to their right, so the plane could hold eight passengers.

"Nice digs," Babette commented. "I wonder who it belongs to?"

"Mac said he borrowed it from someone, and they brought it here last night."

Before another thought could congeal, the plane rumbled beneath their feet, and everyone buckled their seat belts.

"Any food on this ride?" Spider asked.

To be so skinny, the guy packed away a lot of food. Across from Liv, Cal laid his head back and closed his eyes. When the plane was airborne, she placed Misty on the floor, and Babette did the same with Boots.

She finally asked Babette the question burning in her mind. "Why did you insist on Cal coming to New York with us?"

Babette touched Liv's arm. "Liv," she exclaimed in that dramatic fashion of hers, "the man knows everything about dogs. Did you know he helped Rex with the canine program in the prison? They couldn't afford to pay him, but while he had the opportunity, he read everything he could get his hands on about dogs. He is familiar with all the different breeds, their temperaments and habits and history. And let's not even mention he's memorized some major bloodlines. He's a veritable fount of knowledge."

Babette rubbed her pant leg. "I think he deserves a chance. Sometimes life just throws people a curveball, and it takes them a little while to get back on their feet."

Babette took a deep breath. "I'm going to hire him to work for me. The man saved my life." Her last words almost dared Liv to disagree with her decision, but Liv liked her idea.

"I think that's great."

Babette sat back with a huff when she realized she wasn't going to have to defend her decision. "Okay, then."

Liv laid her head back, deciding to rest and refine her plan to take down Mr. Kale once and for all when they arrived in New York. After she'd worked out every angle of her strategy, she closed her eyes and fell asleep.

After the plane landed, everyone climbed out, divided into two groups and hailed taxis to Liv's apartment. Mac assured Liv he thought it was safe since Mr. Kale would assume she was dead, but her home felt small when everyone crowded into the tiny area just inside the door. Cal settled himself on the love seat, and all three dogs followed Babette into the small kitchen area, where she'd feed them and give them some water.

Mac's broad shoulders filled the tiny space as he looked around, and Liv wondered what he thought of her artificial plants scattered throughout the living room and open kitchen area, but she reminded herself she had more important things to worry about.

"Everyone, make yourselves at home." The thought of Mac staying with her in this small space almost made her laugh. She didn't have room for hardly anyone to stay overnight, because there weren't enough sleeping areas. Well, she'd worry about that later. She didn't like to think of Mac leaving, because when this was over and Mr. Kale was behind bars, he would head back to Texas and she would stay in the city.

"I need to talk to you. Alone." His words came out almost harsh, and Liv wondered what that was about, but she had to talk to him, too, and apprise him of her strategy concerning Mr. Kale.

Misty came running from the kitchen, headed straight to the front door and whined. "I have to take Misty out first."

"Wait!" he said, lightly grabbing her arm. "Liv, I have to talk to you. Now. I would have explained on the plane, but you were resting and I didn't want to disturb you. Several men will be here shortly, and I have to explain."

Liv bristled at his commanding tone. "Well, just say it, because when Misty whines that means it's urgent, and she won't use the facilities, so to speak, unless it's me or my neighbor, who cares for her when I'm at work, taking her out."

"I contract out with the FBI."

"What?" she asked, her mind processing the information. Mac was a retired Blue Angel, played the stock market and was a rancher. And then it hit her. "You were hired to investigate me because we're neighbors in Texas and you had a convenient association."

One look at the tic in his jaw and she knew she was right. She almost doubled over when her gut exploded in pain and she couldn't catch her breath. All the kind and sweet things he'd done for her and Misty, even risking his life to save hers, had all been a lie. She was just a...what? A case number to him? At that moment she realized just how deeply she'd tumbled. She'd fallen in love with Mac, even as he was investigating her. Not able to look at him a moment longer, she grabbed Misty off the floor and flung the door open, hoping Mac wouldn't follow her.

Over the pounding in her ears, she heard Babette sternly tell Mac to give Liv a few minutes alone and assured him she would only go right outside the building to let Misty do her business. She took a relieved breath when the elevator doors closed and no one followed her. Holding Misty close as they reached the ground floor, she left the elevator and gave a short nod to the doorman before stumbling outside.

Taking a few deep breaths, she placed Misty at her usual grassy spot near a light pole and tried to regain her equilibrium. It was all a lie. Everything that had passed between her and Mac was a total lie.

Before she had a chance to pick up Misty, two men rapidly approached down the sidewalk, grabbed her by both her arms, dragging her along between them and placed a cloth over her mouth, cutting off her scream. In less than a few seconds, she was shrouded in darkness.

NINETEEN

Mac stood in front of Babette, whose hands were propped on her full hips, her eyes shooting him daggers.

"I can't believe you didn't tell Liv before now that you're with the FBI," she accused. "Are you dense or what? Can't you tell the woman has fallen in love with you?"

"Yeah, man," Spider added after taking a huge bite of a sandwich he'd evidently helped himself to. "You being in the FBI and all, I can't believe you didn't see that one coming," he said while chewing.

His gut felt like it had taken a double punch, and he stood there, frozen. He visualized Liv on the side of the road asking him to take care of her dog as she offered herself up to those two goons so he wouldn't get hurt. Her courage in the plane with the possibility of them crashing had been amazing. And most of all he thought about her willingness to risk her life to save those she cared about. Without warning, all the walls he'd built around his wounded heart crumbled into tiny pieces.

They could work everything else out, because in that one moment of absolute clarity, he knew he'd fallen in love with the fast-talking Texas city girl, and he had to explain everything to her, make her understand that they could overcome all the obstacles keeping them apart.

"I love her," Mac said out loud, his heart near to bursting. "I have to talk to her, make her understand."

Babette nodded her approval. "It's about time. I've watched the two of you dance around each other long enough."

He moved to go after her, but before he could open the door, someone knocked loudly. As he jerked the door open, fear spiked through his system when the harried doorman stood in front of him holding a trembling Misty.

"Two men grabbed Miss Calloway on the sidewalk and kept walking. I saw everything. I called the police, but I'm afraid they'll be too late."

Through a haze of fear, Mac noted Babette's indrawn breath, and he closed his eyes, sending up the most heartfelt prayer he could manage. When he blinked his eyes open, everyone in the room wore horrified expressions, but calmness permeated his very being. Some might call him reckless, but he didn't have time to wait on the police or the FBI agents who were supposed to meet him. She was everything to him, and he was going after her.

Unzipping the duffel bag still sitting at his feet, he grabbed the Search and Rescue vest and called Barnie. Ears flopping as he approached, Barnie came to attention when he spotted the vest and stood still while Mac placed it on him. Opening Liv's small suitcase, which was also on the floor, he pulled out a piece of her clothing and stood.

Spider's eyes rounded in disbelief. "That's how you're gonna find Liv? With that dog?"

"Yes," he said simply and left the apartment.

When they hit the sidewalk, Mac gave Barnie a good sniff of Liv's clothing and said, "Find, Barnie."

Since they were in the city, he put a leash on Barnie. His dog sniffed the ground for a few seconds, then bayed loudly when he caught the scent cone, causing quite a stir on the street. People jumped out of their way when Mac took off running behind his dog.

"Get out of the way," Mac yelled at the people in front of him. When they turned and saw Barnie barreling down the sidewalk, some of them jumped out of the way and others dipped into storefront entrances.

They flew past stores, and about three blocks up, Barnie bayed loudly and turned down a small side street.

They traveled quite a few of the side streets that smelled of refuse, and a homeless man poked his head out of a sleeping bag but disappeared quickly when he saw Barnie coming. Mac stayed alert when they approached three tough-looking guys leaning against the side of a building, but they just stood there, their eyes locked on Barnie as if they'd never seen anything like a dog on a scent.

Mac breathed a sigh of relief when Barnie turned the corner and stopped at the back of an old building that had seen better days. Signaling to Barnie to stop him from baying that he'd found his quarry, Mac paused to catch his breath, then swiftly moved toward the building. The door looked rusted and old.

He turned the knob and prayed it wasn't locked. His

prayer was answered when the door opened with no trouble. "Barnie, off duty. Quiet," he commanded.

The building appeared to have been converted into a store of some sort a very long time ago. A few empty crates were turned over in a corner, and a mouse scurried across the floor. Barnie was too well trained to chase it.

Mac figured there had to be an office somewhere in the building, and he stood still to listen. Faint voices floated from above, and Mac tamped down his fear for Liv. He and Barnie slowly wound their way through the building and up a set of rickety stairs. He followed the voices down a long corridor and backed himself against a wall when he came to a broken-down door that couldn't be closed. Mr. Kale must feel confident that no one could find them here.

Mac's gut clenched in fear when he heard Liv's voice, strong and sure. For the second time, he heard the fear underlying her bravado.

"You're going to kill me anyway. You may as well satisfy my curiosity. Who do you know with enough clout to get those armed drones sent to kill me?"

Mac heard a satisfied, deep chuckle and clenched his fists. The man he assumed to be Kale sounded too sure of himself.

"My dear, I have contacts all over the world. You're just a naive Texas girl attempting to play in a big man's game."

Mac prayed Liv would keep her cool, but Kale's voice changed.

"I want to know more about that Texan who has been protecting you," he demanded in a harsh tone. Mac got ready to spring, even though he didn't know how many men were in the room.

"Are you taking about Mac, Mr. Kale?" Liv asked, sounding surprised. "He's just a cowboy. He doesn't know anything. He allowed me to stay at his ranch. He was simply being neighborly."

Mac fell even more deeply in love with the infuriating woman in there risking her life in order to save his. And in doing so, she'd also confirmed that her boss was the one talking.

"You had a good defense. Why kill the witness against Mr. Stevenson?" Liv prodded.

It was time to put a stop to this before Liv got hurt. They had Kale's goons, who Mac was certain would testify against their boss for reduced sentences. Let the FBI work out the rest. Liv was his only concern.

Mac picked up a piece of wood off the floor and threw it against the opposite wall, praying the noise would be enough to flush out anyone else in the room with Kale. And he braced himself for a fight.

Facing possible death, Liv opened her heart and had just finished the first silent prayer she'd prayed in years when she heard a loud thud in the hall. Mr. Kale's head jerked toward the broken door, and he quickly nodded at the two men who had brought her here. She had a moment's satisfaction when fear crossed Kale's face at the odd noise, but it didn't last long.

She tugged ferociously at the rope tightly binding her hands as the men hurried toward the door. The sound of grunts and blows being exchanged caused her to send up another silent prayer. This one came more naturally than the first one, as if she'd never turned her back on God. As if He had opened His arms and welcomed her back.

The scuffle didn't last long, and Liv's breath caught when Mac limped past the broken door carrying one of the goons' guns. He'd found her! She didn't see Barnie, but she knew he was there, because how else could Mac have tracked her? Liv prayed the dog was okay. Keeping his eyes trained on Mr. Kale, Mac asked Liv, "You okay, honey?"

Fear turned into anger that he'd risked his life for hers. "Do you have anyone with you? If you don't and you came here by yourself, you and I are going to have to have a serious talk, because that was just plain foolish."

One side of his mouth hitched up in a smile, but he kept sharp eyes trained on Kale, who was holding a gun pointed straight at Liv. "Well, now, sweetheart, you'll have a whole lifetime to train me up right after we get married, but I need to have a little chat with your boss right now."

Married? Did Mac just ask her to get married while she had a gun pointed at her? Her heart pounded in joy. But then she realized he was doing the same thing he'd done when he rescued her from a kidnapping on the side of the road—and it was working, based on Mr. Kale's incredulous expression, but Liv understood him well enough to know he was ready to spring into action the moment he got an opening, which she needed to provide. She knew just what to do, and it would only take two words.

"Barnie," she yelled at the top of her lungs, "now!"

Mac's dog came barreling through the broken door

and released the best and loudest bay that Liv had heard yet. It was like the animal knew their lives were at risk. Everything happened at once. Mr. Kale pointed his gun toward the new threat, and Mac pulled the trigger on his own gun, shooting Mr. Kale in the arm, effectively causing her boss's weapon to fly from his fingers and skid across the floor.

Just when Mac got Kale on the floor and pulled his hands behind his back, a horde of men in dark suits swarmed the room with weapons at the ready. They called Mac by name and took possession of Mr. Kale, freeing up Mac. He hurried over to her and untied her hands as quickly as possible.

Facing her, he knelt down and gently rubbed her bruised wrists while raining light kisses on her forehead. "Liv, are you okay? Did they hurt you?" Without giving her time to answer, he pressed her hands against his heart. "Honey, can you ever forgive me? I should have told you I contracted out with the FBI sooner, and I was going to on the plane, but we didn't get a chance to talk. Liv—" he took a deep breath "—I love you, honey, and I want to marry you. Now, don't say anything yet. I know we have some things to work out."

TWENTY

Liv's heart felt near to bursting, as her granddaddy would say. She had made her peace with God, and she loved Mac. Everything else would work itself out. Reclaiming her hands, she framed both sides of his jaw and said, "I love you back," and gave him the sweetest kiss imaginable.

When she pulled back, he grinned. "Well, then."

Liv laughed out loud, even as the men in suits were hauling her boss out of the room, and she repeated his words. "Well, then."

Liv heard an exaggerated throat clearing, and she slapped a hand across her chest when she looked up and saw a man who closely resembled Mac. He grinned at Mac, who was still kneeling in front of her.

"Well, big brother, looks to me as if the lady has literally brought you to your knees."

Liv would have thought Mac would come up swinging, as the Dolan brothers were known to be a rowdy bunch, but he surprised her.

"Sure enough, little brother, sure enough. But what are you doing here?"

He held out a hand to Liv after she and Mac got to their feet. “The name’s Zane Dolan. I work for the Department of Justice, and we’ve had an open investigation into Kale, Kale & Johnston for a while now. I’ve been kept apprised of everything that’s been happening, and we’ll need to get your statement as soon as possible. The agency has taken note of your courage and savviness in this situation.”

Liv’s heart almost stopped. Mac’s brother worked at the DOJ? The endgame in her ten-year career plan? She glanced at Mac, who stood there stoically, waiting to see how she would react. She reached out and took his hand. The smile that blossomed on his face would be imprinted on her mind forever. She loved Mac, but she still hadn’t given up her dream. She was a smart gal, and it was time to figure a few things out.

She looked back at Zane. “It’s so nice to meet you. How did you find us so quickly?”

“The FBI kcpt me informed, and I went with them to your place because I wanted to surprise Mac. We must have gotten there minutes after Mac and Barnie took off after you, because it wasn’t hard to follow your trail. Most people around here won’t soon forget a cowboy and his dog blasting their way through the streets of the city.”

Liv grinned when she pictured Mac and Barnie racing to her rescue, but then she sobered. “What’s going to happen to Mr. Kale?”

Zane’s countenance turned hard. “I’ve spoken to the two goons you captured. It was smart of you to stash them in a small county jail, by the way. They’re willing to testify against your boss for reduced sentences. As far as other, more powerful associates of Mr. Kale, we have eyes on them, and we'll get them sooner or later."

Mac stepped in. "You gonna be home for Easter?"

Zane grinned. "Wouldn't miss it for the world."

Liv watched Mac's brother follow the FBI agents out of the room, and then Mac pulled her into his arms and kissed her. Liv laughed when Barnie nudged them apart, and she reached down and hugged the dog.

"You get two steaks for this day's work, Barnie."

Barnie threw back his head and bayed his heart out.

"We better get back to the apartment. Everyone will be worried." Mac agreed, and they held hands as they made their way through the city streets.

When they arrived back at the apartment, Babette wrapped her arms around Liv and cried all over her shirt. Barnie trotted over to Misty and Boots and licked both small dogs, who in turn curled up against him when he lay on the floor.

When everyone settled down, and Mac and Liv explained everything that had transpired, they all sat there, stunned. Spider even laid his bag of chips aside and stared at Mac with admiration shining out of his eyes.

"Dude, that's some heavy stuff."

Babette shifted a knowing gaze between Liv and Mac, and her eyes filled with both sorrow and happiness. "You're not staying in New York, are you?" she asked Liv.

Everyone in the room stared at them, and Mac pulled

Liv to his side. "If she'll have me, I've asked Liv to marry me."

Babette was the first to move. She hugged Liv, then turned on Mac. "You hurt her and you'll answer to me."

"Yes, ma'am," Mac said through a smile, then added, "I'd like to invite everyone to the ranch for Easter. We always have a big celebration, and there'll be plenty of room for everyone."

Babette wiped a tear from her eye. "Well, you can't take Cal back with you. He's going to work for me."

Liv chuckled when Mac stared at the large man bearing a scarred face, who was lounging on the couch and listening to the proceedings closely.

"Please tell the preacher I appreciate everything he's done for me. If I hadn't come to the ranch, I wouldn't have this job offer. I enjoy working with dogs, and Pastor Dolan gave me the opportunity to learn by helping with the prison canine program."

Mac nodded. "I'll tell him. I'm happy for you."

Babette chimed in, "The man is wonderful with dogs, and he'll be a huge asset to my dog-grooming clinics."

Liv gripped Mac's arm when he slowly said, "Well, now, speaking of your dog clinics, I'm always looking for a new investment. I'd like to see what you've got going here in New York City, Miss Babette."

Liv's heart warmed even more. Mac would make sure Liv and Babette were able to stay close friends.

Spider tried to sidle past them, but Mac caught his arm. "I'll expect to see you at the ranch on Easter."

"Yeah, man, I'll be there. Gotta pick up my car anyway. Just heading home to check on things now that it's safe and all," he said, then slipped out the door and disappeared.

Mac pulled Liv into the kitchen and kissed her again. With his large, callused hands framing her face, he said, "You haven't answered my question. Will you marry me?"

She laid her lips against his and whispered, "Yes, I'll marry you, Mac Dolan."

They sealed the commitment with the sweetest of kisses, and Mac pulled back and looked down at her. "You have a lot of things to wrap up here in New York with the Kale case, and me and Barnie are heading back to Texas, but I'll call you every night until Easter. We have a lot of things to discuss, but we'll figure everything out."

Liv lifted her chin for one more kiss, and Mac removed Barnie's vest, grabbed his duffel and was out the door. An hour later Babette had taken Cal and Boots back to her apartment, and Liv and Misty were alone. She lay in bed that night and thought about everything that had transpired and what the future would hold.

She prayed, then opened her eyes with a smile when a perfect solution to her career presented itself.

Standing on the side of the small airstrip that would bring Liv back into his arms, Mac groused as his rowdy brothers almost knocked him down while pushing each other and roughhousing. It didn't matter how old they were—whenever they got together, it was as if they reverted back to their childhood. The rowdy Dolan boys, everyone called them while they were growing up. The only one missing was Dean, and everyone was worried about the youngest Dolan, off fighting a war in a foreign country. But today was a day of celebration. Mac would get in touch with Dean soon enough.

The plane he'd sent to pick up Liv came into sight, and his heart started thumping—or maybe that was his brothers slapping him on the back. It seemed like it took forever, but the aircraft finally landed and the door opened. He would have flown there and picked her up himself, but he'd spent the time getting his new house finished for her arrival and he'd cut it close.

Mac ran to the steps as soon as they hit the ground and climbed them two at a time. Liv was inside gathering her things, and he swept her into his arms. His brothers cheered as he carried her down the steps.

When he placed her on her feet, his brothers surrounded her, each taking turns smooching her cheek. Mac called a halt to the proceedings among much laughter and kidding. His brothers were ecstatic that he'd found someone to love.

Spider, whom Mac had sent word to meet Liv at the airport to hitch a ride to Texas, had exited the plane at some point with Misty in his arms and came up beside Mac. "Man, what do you people eat around here?"

It took Mac a second to realize Spider was talking about how tall and large Mac and his brothers were. "Clean living, Spider, nothing but clean living."

Barnie was dancing around but sat right down in front of Liv when she asked him to. All his brothers became interested in the proceedings when she shook out an article of clothing she had in her hand.

"Barnie, Babette made something very special for

you." She velcroed something around the dog's neck and smoothed it over his back. "It's a hero's cape."

Mac grinned, and Barnie threw back his head and bayed. Everyone was enjoying the moment, and Mac was surprised when Zane approached Liv with serious intent on his face.

"Liv," Zane said, "I've talked with all my associates at the Department of Justice, and we agreed to offer you a junior position. You'll have to work your way up, but you'll have a foot in the door."

Mac was stunned, and his first response was to sock his brother for making a somewhat complicated matter even more complicated, but deep down, he wanted Liv to have her dream. He and Liv had talked every night on the phone since he left the city, but she'd refused to make any major decisions until they could talk in person. Mac took a deep breath. He wanted Liv to be happy above all things, and he watched her closely to see her response to something she'd wanted her entire career.

She graced Zane with a radiant smile and said, "Well, now, I'm honored by such a wonderful offer, and I'd love to be a part of the DOJ team in Alpine. That's close to Brewster County and would be perfect."

Mac's heart soared. He grabbed her by the hand and pulled her away from the group of men. Barnie and Misty, who were dancing around their feet now, followed them. This was the beginning of the rest of their lives. "We have just enough time for you to see our new house before Patsy rounds everyone up for Easter dinner and I introduce you to the folks."

Like two giddy children, they left everyone behind

with the dogs following them, but both of them laughed when Zane's voice floated on the air behind them.

"Spider—I understand that's your online pseudonym. We've been watching you, and I think it'd be to your benefit to come to work for us, unless you'd like us to delve a little deeper into your activities..."

Mac and Liv looked at each other. They started laughing, and Mac grabbed her hand. Pulling her forward, he thought about their future and halted in his tracks. Everything was perfect, but there was something they hadn't discussed. Something near and dear to his heart.

"Mac, what is it?" Liv asked, worry lacing her words.

He took both her hands, and they faced each other. "Liv, I love you, but do you want kids?" he blurted out, and he held his breath until she spoke.

"Well, now, cowboy, I think you're asking the wrong question."

He did his best to slip into his Texas routine, but it fell flat. "And what question should I be asking?"

"How many?"

"What?"

"The question shouldn't have been whether I want to have kids, but how many."

Mac felt his lips stretch into a smile as wide as Texas. "Well, then, Miss Calloway, how many kids would you like to have?"

She propped a slim hand on her hip and mimicked a Texas drawl. "It seems to me that Brewster County would be a mighty boring place without another pack of rowdy Dolan kids coming along."

Mac swooped her off her feet and kissed her before

setting her down. “Let’s go see if we have enough room in that house I built for all those kids.”

The dogs pranced around the happy couple as they finally made their way home.

* * * * *

If you enjoyed Texas Ranch Refuge*,*
pick up these other thrilling stories from Liz Shoaf:

Betrayed Birthright
Identity: Classified
Holiday Mountain Conspiracy
Texas Ranch Sabotage

Available now from Love Inspired Suspense!

Find more great reads at www.LoveInspired.com

Dear Reader,

One reason you'll always find dogs in my books is because I'm very active in dog sports, specifically agility and herding, and I *love* working with dogs. Dog training is a long and arduous process. It takes a ton of patience but produces lots of smiles when you and your dog finally get it and become a team. I hope you enjoy Mac and Liv's story, along with their very interesting Search and Rescue bluetick coonhound and tiny papillon. Oh, and there's a toy poodle who makes an appearance, but you'll have to read the book to find out more about her. :)

I'd love to hear from you. You can reach me through my website: www.lizshoaf.com.

Happy reading!
Liz Shoaf

COMING NEXT MONTH FROM
Love Inspired Suspense

FOLLOWING THE TRAIL
K-9 Search and Rescue • by Lynette Eason

Lacey Jefferson's search for her missing sister quickly turns into a murder investigation, thrusting Lacey and her search-and-rescue dog, Scarlett, into a killer's sights. Now teaming up with her ex-boyfriend, Sheriff Creed Payne, might be the only way to discover the murderer's identity—and survive.

SECRET SABOTAGE
by Terri Reed

Ian Delaney is determined to uncover who sabotaged his helicopter and caused the crash that left him with no memory. But he's convinced his family-appointed bodyguard, Simone Walker, will only get in his way. Can they learn to work together and unravel deadly secrets...before they're hunted down?

SNOWBOUND AMISH SURVIVAL
by Mary Alford

When armed men burst into her patient's house looking for *her*, Amish midwife Hope Christner barely escapes with her pregnant friend. But as the assailants chase them through the woods in a blizzard, Hope's only choice is to turn to Hunter Shetler, the nearest neighbor—and her ex-fiancé.

UNDERCOVER MOUNTAIN PURSUIT
by Sharon Dunn

After witnessing a shooting in a remote location, high-risk photographer Willow Farris races to help—and runs into her old flame, Quentin Decker. Undercover to take down an international smuggler, Quentin has a mission to complete. But to bring the criminals to justice, he and Willow have to get off the mountain alive...

LETHAL CORRUPTION
by Jane M. Choate

Prosecuting a gang leader is the biggest case of deputy district attorney Shannon DeFord's career—if she lives through the trial. With nobody else to trust, Shannon must accept protection from security operative Rafe Zuniga. But when a larger conspiracy is exposed, someone will do anything to keep the truth buried.

COVERT TAKEDOWN
by Kathleen Tailer

With her ex's WITSEC cover blown and someone trying to murder him, it falls to FBI agent Tessa McIntyre to protect the man who left her at the altar. But can she and Gabriel Grayson put their past aside long enough to catch a killer...and ensure they have a chance at a future?

LOOK FOR THESE AND OTHER LOVE INSPIRED BOOKS WHEREVER BOOKS ARE SOLD, INCLUDING MOST BOOKSTORES, SUPERMARKETS, DISCOUNT STORES AND DRUGSTORES.

LISCNM0122A

Lacey Jefferson's search for her missing sister quickly turns into a murder investigation, thrusting Lacey and her search-and-rescue dog, Scarlett, into a killer's sights. Now teaming up with her ex-boyfriend, Sheriff Creed Payne, might be the only way to discover the murderer's identity—and survive.

Read on for a sneak peek of Following the Trail *by Lynette Eason, available February 2022 from Love Inspired Suspense.*

Had he really just offered employment to the woman who'd broken his heart? There was no way he wanted to be stuck working with her day in and day out, a constant reminder of how she'd chosen the big city over him—over them. Then again, she could accuse him of doing the same thing to her.

But that was different. This was his home.

And hers, too, whether she wanted to admit it or not.

"Seriously," he found himself saying, "it would be full-time with benefits and everything."

"As what, Creed?"

"A deputy. And leader of the K-9 unit."

"You don't have a K-9 unit."

"We would if you started one."

She gaped at him. "I need to talk to you about Fawn, but first I have something I need to take care of."

"What?"

"Scarlett was real antsy around that fallen tree trunk," she said. "I want to go take a look at what she was reacting so strongly to."

Creed nodded. "I'll go out there with you, and we can talk on the way."

Lacey studied him for a moment, then gave a short dip of her head. "Can you keep Regina and the others here until we finish checking out that tree trunk?" she asked.

He narrowed his eyes. "Why? Don't tell me Scarlett is trained in cadaver search, as well."

Lacey shook her head. "She started out that way but hated it and was terrible at it. She apparently just really did not like the smell and would be very skittish when she got close to a dead body."

"Can't say I blame her," he muttered.

"And she would sneeze. She was acting that way out by the tree."

Creed froze. "I see. And you think there's a dead body out there?"

"I don't think so, I'm…afraid so."

LISEXP0122-A